"A kil

"It was a long time ago," Lauren pointed out to Seth. "If there was a killer out there, he's gone."

"Not necessarily," Seth said. "There's a chance he stuck around. It's a realistic thought."

"Maybe," she said. "Or maybe it's just your way of getting what you want."

"What I want is you safe. That's all there is to it."

"There's never an *all there is to it* with you, Seth. There's only wanting more, different, better. As soon as you get one thing, you're off looking for the next." Lauren's face heated. "I'm sorry. That was uncalled for."

"No, it wasn't," he said. "But it wasn't the truth, either. You've changed, Lauren. So have I."

* * *

REUNION REVELATIONS: Secrets surface when old friends—and foes—get together.

Books by Shirlee McCoy

Love Inspired Suspense

Die Before Nightfall #5
Even in the Darkness #14
When Silence Falls #18
Little Girl Lost #40
Valley of Shadows #61
Stranger in the Shadows #76
Missing Persons #88

Steeple Hill Trade

Still Waters

SHIRLEE McCOY

has always loved making up stories. As a child, she daydreamed elaborate tales in which she was the heroine—gutsy, strong and invincible. Though she soon grew out of her superhero fantasies, her love for storytelling never diminished. She knew early that she wanted to write inspirational fiction, and she began writing her first novel when she was a teenager. Still, it wasn't until her third son was born that she truly began pursuing her dream of being published. Three years later she sold her first book. Now a busy mother of four, Shirlee is a homeschool mom by day and an inspirational author by night. She and her husband and children live in Maryland and share their house with a dog and a guinea pig. You can visit her Web site at www.shirleemccoy.com.

Missing Persons

SHIRLEE MCCOY

Steeple
Hill®

Published by Steeple Hill Books™

Special thanks and acknowledgment are given to Shirlee McCoy for her contribution to the REUNION REVELATIONS miniseries.

STEEPLE HILL BOOKS

Steeple
Hill®

ISBN-13: 978-0-373-44278-2
ISBN-10:   0-373-44278-5

MISSING PERSONS

www.SteepleHill.com

Printed in U.S.A.

And now these three remain: faith, hope and love.
But the greatest of these is love.
—*1 Corinthians* 13:13

To Emma Grace, daughter and ally in our house filled with men—I love you just because you're you.

And to Jessica Alvarez, editor extraordinaire, who helped make sense of this wonderful continuity. Thanks!

PROLOGUE

She wasn't angry. She wasn't even mildly annoyed.

And Lauren Owens figured if she told herself that enough times she just might believe it.

Okay. Maybe *angry* wasn't the right word. Maybe *irritated* was a better fit. *Perturbed. Frustrated.*

She only had herself to blame. She'd been such a pushover. Why hadn't she refused when Steff asked her to participate in the Magnolia College fund-raiser dinner and auction?

Because she hadn't wanted to disappoint her friend, that's why. Instead, she'd managed to add two very unwanted complications to her already complicated life.

Seth.

His son.

Her hands tightened on the steering wheel of her Mustang convertible, the blackness of the night beyond the car's headlights reflecting her dark mood.

Up ahead, her sister Deandra's house beckoned, a light shining in an upstairs window spilling out into the darkness. Dee was probably waiting for a rehash of the evening's events. Unfortunately, that would have to wait. Lauren wasn't in the mood to talk.

She pulled around to the back of the house, following the driveway to the small converted carriage house at the edge of the property. Trees loomed over it, dark shadows against the night sky, hulking figures that looked like giant men waiting for the unwary to step beneath their grasping arms. Lauren shivered, her gaze riveted to the front of the carriage house. She'd left the light above the front door on, but it was out now, the large bushes on either side casting deep gray shadows over what should have been a well-lit area.

A warning raced along her spine and lodged at the base of her skull, but she ignored it. Bad things didn't happen in small-town Georgia.

Didn't they?

The question whispered through her mind as she stepped out of the Mustang and started toward the door. A woman had died in Magnolia Falls, her body hidden for ten years and just recently found during Magnolia College's library renovations. That was proof enough that bad things did indeed happen in small towns. But that was a long time ago and right here, right now a burned-out lightbulb was more likely the cause of the darkened stoop than some faceless, nameless murderer.

Right?

A breeze brushed against her hair as she moved toward the carriage house, ghostly fingers that trailed along her skin and made her shiver. She could almost imagine someone watching from the darkened windows or shadowy corners. Almost hear the raspy breath of the watcher.

"Stop it!" She hissed the words, refusing to allow the timid mousy creature she'd once been to take hold. Ten years living alone, ten years building her reputation as a premier Savannah chef, ten years learning who she was and where she belonged had made her strong. Independent. A woman who didn't panic, didn't overreact, and did not allow her imagination to get the better of her.

She shoved open the carriage house door, flicked on the living room light and froze. Shredded fabric. White stuffing pulled from once-pristine sofa and chairs. Books strewn across paint-splattered hardwood floor. Framed photos trampled and torn. To the left, the bathroom door yawned open, light spilling across the floor and reflecting off a slick, wet substance that might have been shampoo, lotion. Blood. To the right, the lone bedroom door was closed. She'd left it open. She was sure of it.

A sound drifted into the silence. The pad of feet on carpet. The brush of a hand against the wall. Lauren didn't wait to hear more. She stumbled backward, away from the subtle sound and from the chaos. Then turned and ran toward Dee's house and safety.

ONE

Late summer painted the sky in shades of gold and purple, the setting sun sliding toward the horizon in a final blaze of light as Lauren eased out of her sister's car and smoothed her hand over the simple lines of her black cocktail dress. "Ready or not, here we go."

"I'm definitely ready, but you look like you're going to chicken out." Dee's words held a hint of humor, but her gaze was somber as she rounded the car and put a hand on Lauren's arm.

"Chicken out of what? It's just a dinner."

"And an auction."

"Which I said I'd participate in."

"And which we both know you regretted doing two seconds after the fact."

It was true and Lauren didn't bother denying it. Her older sister knew her too well to be fooled by anything she might say. "It's not that I don't want to help raise funds for

Magnolia College. It's just that this stuff isn't my thing. I'd rather not have all the attention."

"You'd rather let other people take center stage while you hide in a back room somewhere." Dee smiled, her perfectly applied makeup showcasing flawless skin and vivid blue eyes—the only feature the two sisters had in common. Pretty and popular in high school and college, Dee had never seemed to mind being in the spotlight. Lauren always had.

"There's nothing wrong with that."

"No, but this will be good for you and good for your business. Just think of all the clients you'll gain."

"I don't need any more clients. I'm busy enough." Her personal chef business had taken off in the past year, word of mouth expanding her clientele enough that she was considering hiring another chef.

"Then skip out. I can tell Steff you're not feeling well. You can go back to my place and chill. Come back and pick me up when the fund-raiser is over."

"You know I can't do that."

"I know you *won't* do it, which is why there's no sense standing around here talking about it any longer." Dee tightened her hold on Lauren's arm and started toward the door of Mossy Oak Inn.

Lauren wanted to pull back, take a minute to study the people moving in groups toward the entrance. She wanted to search their faces, looking for the one person she didn't want to see. If he wasn't there, she'd be fine. If he was...

She'd still be fine.

After all, she'd agreed to participate in the auction knowing that Seth Chartrand might be there. That's exactly what she intended to do. If that meant coming face-to-face with a past she'd just as soon forget, so be it.

A few yards ahead, two women and three men neared the door, laughing and talking, their easy camaraderie drawing Lauren's attention. The tall broad-shouldered man walking just a step ahead of the rest kept it. Purposeful stride, taller than the other two men, he had an easy confidence that made Lauren slow her pace and pull against Dee's hold.

Maybe she wasn't as ready to face Seth as she thought she was.

Dee shot her a look, raising one perfectly arched eyebrow. "Relax. That's not Seth."

"I didn't think it was."

"Sure you did, but you don't have to worry about running into the jerk. He never attends alumni events. Probably too embarrassed to show his face after what he did to you."

"What happened between Seth and me happened eleven years ago, Dee. We're both over it now, so there's no need to call him a jerk."

Dee shrugged slender shoulders. "Any guy who talks marriage with my sister and then breaks her heart will always be a jerk to me."

Lauren laughed, her sister's support easing some of her anxiety. She still didn't want to see Seth tonight. Jerk or not, he had been a huge part of her high school years. Their breakup during college had been heart shattering. It had also forced her to grow up and face the world alone.

But that wasn't something she wanted to worry about tonight. Tonight she wanted to relax and enjoy the company of old friends, the ease of having no clients to cook for, no menus to plan. She refused to let anxiety about seeing Seth ruin that for her.

Dee tugged her across the parking lot, pulling her along at a swift pace, her perfume wafting on cool September air, her stride brisk and confident despite the high heels she wore. Lauren's own heels threatened to trip her up and send her spilling onto the pavement. "Slow down, Dee. You know I can't walk fast in these shoes."

"You can't walk fast in anything higher than a tennis shoe, but I forgive you. Now, hurry up before we miss something good."

"Like what? Two hundred people all gossiping about someone just out of earshot?"

"Not someone. The skeleton that was found near the library. That's all anyone in Magnolia Falls is talking about lately."

"Yeah? It sounds like a pretty morbid topic for dinner conversation."

"Morbid doesn't bother people nowadays. They want information and they don't care how or when they get it. The more they have, the more important they feel."

"What's to feel important about? That poor woman's death has nothing to do with anyone here tonight."

"We'll see. I plan to find out what people are saying, what they're thinking. How it's going to affect Magnolia College." An employee at a successful public relations firm, Dee was always interested in how information could affect the reputation of organizations. It didn't surprise Lauren that her sister was interested in hearing what was being said about the human remains that had been found on Magnolia College's campus.

Lauren, on the other hand, cared more about the menu than the gossip. Balance and aesthetics, temperature, taste, those things could be controlled and predicted. *People* could not. "I don't see how something that happened years ago could have any effect on the college."

"How could it not? Finding a body on campus is sure to bring bad publicity. It already has. You've seen the papers. All the talk about safety on campus and whether or not Magnolia College is doing enough to make sure its students are protected from predators." Dee was moving even faster now, her body nearly humming with excitement and energy. It had been that vibrancy that had made her popular in high school and college, and still made her the center of any gathering.

"I thought all publicity was good publicity."

"Maybe if you're an actress. What parent is going to want to send a son or daughter to a school where a body lay buried and unnoticed for ten years?"

"Good point. I guess that's why you're a publicist and I'm a chef." Lauren pushed opened double-wide doors and stepped into the warmth of the inn. Muted light illuminated the spacious foyer and gleamed off rich mahogany furniture. The elegant simplicity made it *the* place to be, and most high-class Magnolia Falls functions were held there.

"You're here! I was worried you weren't going to show." Stephanie Kessler hurried toward them, blond hair bouncing as she moved, violet eyes reflecting both worry and relief.

"Have you ever known me to not do something I said I

would?" Lauren smiled and leaned forward to embrace her friend.

"No, but the way things have been going lately, I wouldn't have been surprised if you broke with tradition."

"The way things have been going lately? It seems to me they've been going pretty well for you. You've met the man of your dreams and are desperately in love. What could be better?" Dee air kissed Steff's cheeks.

"Being in love and not having to worry about things at the college." Steff smiled, but it didn't reach her eyes.

"You're always worrying about that."

"Now more so than ever." Steff glanced around, then spoke quietly. "I'm getting enough e-mail to crash my computer and phone calls all day long. Someone's body was under that sidewalk. Everyone wants to know whose." She shook her head.

"The police aren't any closer to identifying the remains?"

"No, but I can't help wondering—"

"If it's someone we knew." Lauren had been wondering the same.

"There were a lot of people missing at the reunion. Payton Bell. Josie Skerritt. Angela Heaton." She shrugged, turned toward the corridor that led to the ballroom. "I guess now isn't the time to talk about it. Dinner's going to be served soon. Then the auction. You're up first, Lauren."

"Up first?"

"I'll introduce you and the service you're offering. All you need to do is stand there and look gorgeous while people bid."

"Gorgeous is more Dee's thing than mine."

"Give yourself a little credit, Laur. You look beautiful.

Even if you can't walk in those shoes." Dee smirked and hurried down the corridor with Steff.

Leaving Lauren no choice but to follow.

She walked more slowly, her wobbly heels twisting under her as she headed for the ballroom muttering under her breath. "If I make it through tonight without falling on my face and completely embarrassing myself it'll be a miracle."

"Still talk to yourself? I thought you'd have outgrown the habit by now." The gruff voice came from behind her, deep, quiet and filled with humor and warmth. And a million memories Lauren refused to acknowledge.

"Seth." She schooled her features as she turned to face him, pasting on the cool, professional smile she'd perfected over the years. "I wondered if you'd be here tonight. It's been a long time."

"It has been. So long I wondered if you'd even remember me." He looked the same, but older. The fine lines at the corner of his eyes, the serious expression in his gaze speaking of a maturity and depth he hadn't had when he'd been a young, brash high school student, or a law-school-bound young adult.

When he'd been the man she'd put her hopes and dreams in. The man she'd loved.

"How could I forget?" The words slipped out, and Seth smiled, the slow, deliberate curve doing exactly what it had the first time they'd met—weakening Lauren's knees, speeding her pulse, muddling her thoughts. Fortunately, it was eleven years and a broken heart too late for her to feel more than mild surprise at her reaction. "What I mean is—"

"I know what you mean. It's hard to forget what we had."

"And how it ended."

"That, too." He smiled again. "Are you here with your sister? Or do you need a dinner companion?"

Was that an invitation? If so, Lauren had no intention of acknowledging it. "I'm here with Dee and a few friends."

"Let me guess—Steff, Jen, Cassie and Kate."

"That's right."

"Then I'd better get you inside the ballroom before they miss you and come looking." He reached for her arm, but Lauren sidestepped, avoiding his touch. Seeing him was bad enough. Feeling the warmth of his hand would be a hundred times worse.

"I can manage on my own. Thanks."

His gaze locked with hers, then dropped to the simple black cocktail dress she wore. She'd planned her wardrobe to reflect how she wanted to portray herself—elegant, in charge, independent. Strong. Much different than the shy young woman she'd been in high school and college.

Maybe he saw that. Surprise flashed in his eyes. Then speculation, as if he were trying to match the woman he was speaking to with the one he'd known so long ago. "I'm sure you can. It was nice seeing you again."

She nodded, but didn't say the same. Nice wasn't the word she'd use. Uncomfortable. Strange. Even a little alarming. Not nice.

"Lola?"

She'd already turned away, but his voice, the pet name he'd used so often when they were young stopped her in her tracks. "Don't call me that, Seth."

"Why not? It's how I think of you."

"I'd rather you not think of me at all."

"That's a little cold." He moved up beside her, relaxed and at ease. Confident. Just as he'd always been.

"I didn't mean it to be. I just meant that we stopped thinking about each other years ago. There's no reason to start again."

He stared into her eyes for a minute, searching for something. Forgiveness? Acceptance? Neither was Seth's style. At least it hadn't been.

Finally, he nodded. "Point taken."

"Good. Now I really had better go find my sister and friends. Enjoy your evening." She smiled, hoping he wouldn't see how shaken she felt, how off balance. Seeing Seth had been harder than she'd thought it would be, but it was over and the rest of the evening could only get better. Right?

Right.

Except for the part where she'd have to stand up in front of the ballroom while people bid for her chef services. And the part where she'd have to explain to Dee and the other girls why it had taken so long to get to their table. Not to mention the whole being-in-a-room-filled-with-people-she-didn't-know thing.

At least she'd have Dee and the gang close by. They were always good for conversation, laughs and distraction. For now, she'd let that be enough.

TWO

Lauren had changed. That much was obvious. Seth watched as she moved to the front of the ballroom and took her place next to Steff, her fitted black dress hugging slender curves and long lean lines. Dark hair, longer than she'd worn in high school or college, fell past her shoulders in thick waves. She hadn't tried to tame it as she had so often when she was younger. That in itself was a surprise. What surprised Seth more was her direct gaze, the confident way she held herself, smiling out at the crowd as if she enjoyed being there.

And maybe she did.

Seth had certainly grown and changed during the past decade. It shouldn't surprise him that Lauren had, as well. Somehow, though, it did. When he'd heard that she'd be offering a week's worth of her services as a personal chef at the auction, he'd wondered what it would be like to see her again, had wondered if she'd be married or single, changed or the same. He'd pictured her in loose sweaters and baggy jeans, hair pulled away from a pale makeup free face. He'd thought she'd stand quietly in the background, a little mousy, a little shy. What he hadn't imagined was the self-assured professional she'd become, the stunning beauty she no longer tried to hide. Where she'd once been content to hide in the shadows of her sister's popularity, she now seemed determined to shine, her understated sophistication exactly what Seth would have expected from any other woman in her profession.

He just hadn't expected it from her.

As if she sensed his thoughts, she turned her head, scanning the tables, her gaze drifting from person to person and finally coming to rest on Seth. For a moment, their gazes held, a million memories passing between them. Then she looked away, her smile fading just a bit, some of the animation and vitality seeping from her expression.

He'd done that to her. And a lot worse. Though, as she'd said earlier, that had been years ago. He'd apologized for the way he'd broken off their relationship and then he'd put it behind him.

At least he'd thought he had.

"You're going to bid on this aren't you?" The stage whisper came from Jeannine Maynard, a retired employee of Magnolia College and Seth's busybody neighbor. She'd been the one to tell him about the renowned chef from Savannah who planned to auction off a week's worth of allergen-free meals.

"It's why I came, Ms. Jeannine."

"Then get to it before the auctioneer closes the bid and you lose out."

Seth raised his card, topping the previous bid and noting the slight widening of Lauren's eyes. She wasn't happy, but he hadn't expected her to be. Unfortunately for both of them, Seth's son Jake's dietary needs took precedence over anything else.

"You're going to pay a pretty penny if you want to win this one, Seth. Quite a crowd showed up tonight."

"There's no surprise there." An older gentleman seated next to Jeannine spoke up. "Everyone is hoping there'll be some mention of the investigation into the body that was found at the college."

"Skeleton. Not body. Buried under the sidewalk of all things. You'd think someone would have noticed while they were pouring the cement." Jeannine flashed her own card, upping the bid and smirking at Seth.

"Not if the body was under a layer of dirt." Seth flashed his card again, caught Lauren's glare, but chose to ignore it.

"Do they have any idea whose body it was?" The woman across the table leaned in, her eyes wide behind thick-lensed glasses.

"If they do they aren't saying." Seth flashed his card again, driving the bid higher.

"From what I hear, they think it's a woman. Young. Maybe a student who was attending the college." Jeannine spoke quietly, and everyone at the table leaned toward her. Except for Seth. He'd heard the information before, had spent way too much of his time speculating about who it could be. A woman. Someone who'd disappeared ten years ago.

Ellen.

His half sister and his parents had had a big blowup the year Jake was born. Ellen had stormed out of the house and never returned.

That had been ten years ago. About the same time the first renovations had been done on Magnolia College's library. About the same time the sidewalk had been poured. She'd had friends in Magnolia Falls and a job doing freelance photography for the public relations department at Magnolia College. And now she was gone.

Seth flashed his number again, trying to block out the conversation and his own morbid thoughts. Sure Ellen had had a lot of friends in Magnolia Falls. It was possible she'd visited there after the blowup with their parents, but that didn't mean she had. It certainly didn't mean her body had been hidden under a sidewalk for the past ten years.

Seth bid a final time, winning Lauren's chef services and then following her progress as she made her way through the crowded room. She took a seat at her table, whispering to her sister, Deandra, who wasn't quite as restrained. She shot Seth a look filled with malice. Obviously, she wasn't going to let bygones be bygones. Jennifer, Cassie and Kate were at the table, too, and glanced in Seth's direction before leaning forward and beginning what looked like an animated conversation.

They could talk all they wanted. Seth had accomplished his goal. The only person he had to explain things to was Lauren, and he'd have plenty of time to do that while they worked on the menu for Jake. As for the rest of the ladies, they'd just have to hear the details from her.

Steff announced the next item up for auction and another bidding war began. This one over a summer's worth of lawn service. Lauren's sister made a bid, the woman next to her saying something that made the rest of the table laugh. As Lauren's companions turned their attention to other things, Lauren whispered something in Deandra's ear, grabbed a small handbag from the floor and stood, moving quickly toward the door and out of the room.

Five minutes passed, then ten as Seth tried to convince

himself not to follow. He didn't do a good job of it and finally gave up the effort, pushing back his chair and standing.

"Are you leaving already?" Jeannine looked up from a dinner roll she was slathering with butter.

"Just going to call and make sure my son isn't giving the babysitter grief. I'll be back in a few minutes."

"As if that sweet young man could ever give anyone trouble."

"I won't tell him you called him sweet." Seth strode away from the table.

The lobby was empty, the sounds of laughter drifting in from the events room barely disturbing the refined air the inn worked so hard to maintain. He pulled his cell phone from his pocket, dialing his home number as he stepped outside into cool September air, his gaze scanning the parking lot.

"Hello?"

"Hi, Reese. It's Seth."

"Is everything okay?" Reese sounded as bubbly as ever. Apparently her ten-year-old charge hadn't worn her out yet.

"Everything is fine. I just thought I'd check in. Make sure my son wasn't giving you trouble about his bedtime."

"You know he is. He wants more time to read the book I brought him." A junior at Magnolia College, Reese had been Jake's babysitter for two years. Seth had come to value her dependability. Being a single parent was hard. Having reliable child care made things easier.

"How much time do you plan to give him?"

"You know me too well. Is a half hour okay?"

"Works for me, but tell him that if he values tomorrow's fishing trip, he'd better not push for more."

"I will. See you when you get home." The phone clicked as Reese disconnected, and Jake shook his head, smiling a little as he thought of his son and Reese conspiring to extend Jake's bedtime. Dependable or not, Reese wasn't nearly as far from her childhood as Seth was from his. That made her more likely to allow later bedtimes and extra snacks. Which was fine with Seth.

Once in a while.

And that was as frequently as he went out. According to Jeannine and a few other well-meaning neighbors and church ladies that wasn't nearly enough, but Seth wasn't in the market for a relationship. One marriage was enough for a lifetime.

He pushed aside the thought and the memories that went with it, and turned back toward the inn. That's when he saw her—sitting on a bench near the corner of the building, her shoulders slumped, her dark hair spilling forward to cover her face. Lola. Despite what she said, despite what she wanted, that's how he thought of Lauren. The nickname was one he'd coined when he'd met her his sophomore year of high school. A transplant from New Orleans, Lauren had seemed lost and alone as she wandered through the cafeteria of their Savannah high school. When she'd glanced his way and offered a sweet smile, Seth's adolescent heart had melted. Despite his determination to keep the past at bay, the memories washed over him, bittersweet in their simplicity.

"You new?"

"Yes. I'm Lauren Owens. From Louisiana."

"Well, Lauren Owens from Louisiana, it looks like you could use a friend. I'm Seth Chartrand. Want to have lunch with me?"

"I was looking for my sister."

"No problem, Lola, I'll help you find her. We can all have lunch together."

Even now, the memory made him smile. Friendship had blossomed that day. From there love had grown. Unfortunately, Seth hadn't known enough about life to value it. He liked to tell himself he'd matured since then. Sometimes he almost believed it.

He moved toward her, grass and leaves crackling beneath his feet, the sweet scent of newly mown lawn heavy in the air. "You look like you could use a friend."

She tensed, but didn't turn toward him. "No. Just some fresh air."

"I guess that makes two of us." He kept his words casual, ignoring her not so subtle dismissal.

"You shouldn't have followed me out here, Seth."

"Who said I did?"

"Didn't you?"

"I thought you might like an explanation."

"As long as you have the money to pay for what you bought, no explanation is necessary." She stood, moving a few steps away, her lean form taut with whatever she was feeling. Eleven years ago he would have known, would have been able to read the look in her eyes, the expression on her face. Now she was a puzzle he couldn't quite solve.

"Maybe not, but I'm going to give you one anyway. My son has severe food allergies, Lauren. Making meals he can eat and enjoy is difficult. I thought learning from an expert in the field might make his life easier."

She nodded, but there was no softening in her expression. "You'll have to make me a list of what he's allergic to. I'll put together meal ideas based on that. Do you have an e-mail address where I can send the menu?"

"Sure." He pulled out a business card and handed it to her. "I'll call you tomorrow with the list of allergens."

"It'll be easier if you e-mail it to me." She handed him her card, and Seth glanced down at her e-mail and business address. Savannah. She hadn't moved far from home. At least in this she hadn't surprised him. The Lauren he'd dated had always been content to be near home and family.

He, on the other hand, had been desperate for adventure and freedom.

"How does this work? Do I come to you? Or will you come to me?"

"Once the menu is agreed on, I'll come to your house to prepare the food."

"That's a lot of miles on your car."

"I'll do the week's worth of cooking in one visit." She shrugged. "Even if I didn't, it wouldn't be a big deal. I'm staying with Dee for the next two weeks."

"Vacation?"

"And favor. Steff asked me to take part in the auction. I agreed. Driving back and forth between Savannah and Magnolia Falls didn't make sense. I figured I'd do the job, then take some time to relax."

"Dee's not in town, is she?" If she was, she must stay close to home. Seth had yet to run into her.

"No, but she's close enough." She smiled and it was the same sweet curve of her lips he'd noticed the first time he'd seen her.

"You haven't changed, Lola."

"The fact that you say that just proves how little you know about me." She ran a hand over loose curls, avoiding eye contact. "I'd better head back in."

He should let her go. She was right after all. He didn't know her. But he did know that tonight had to be as uncomfortable for her as it was for him. Seeing each other after all these years, trying hard not to remember the way things had been, the way they had ended. If it was hard for him, it must be doubly difficult for Lauren.

Before she could walk away, he put his hand on her arm, feeling firm muscles beneath silky fabric. "I'm sorry if my winning your services is uncomfortable for you."

"Tonight was about raising funds for Magnolia College. As long as I've helped do that, I'm not uncomfortable with the outcome."

"You're sure?"

"Of course. I think we're both professional enough to keep the past where it belongs."

"Professional enough? Sure. But that doesn't change the facts."

"What facts, Seth? That we dated years ago? That you broke up with me? That same story plays out a million times a year with a million couples. It's not something we need to make an issue of."

Maybe they didn't, but it *was* an issue for Seth. Being near Lauren brought back memories he'd spent a long time trying to forget. Maybe tonight was about more than Jake and his food allergies. Maybe it was about making amends. Not that that was possible. He'd broken Lauren's heart, laughed at her dreams, calling them boring and mundane. Just thinking about it was enough to make him cringe.

"The past is still between us. Whether we make an issue of it or not."

"Look, Seth—"

Seth's cell phone rang, interrupting her words. He glanced at the number, his chest tightening with worry. Reese didn't call unless there was a problem. "It's my son's babysitter. I've got to take this."

Lauren moved a few steps away, but didn't return to the inn. "Hello?"

"Seth, it's Reese. Jacob's having a reaction to something. He's breathing okay, but I think you'd better come home."

"Did he have anything to eat besides what I left for him?"

"Nothing."

"Are you certain?" He started toward his car, his stomach clenching with anxiety. Jake's reactions ranged from mild to severe depending on the allergen.

"If he had anything else, he's not admitting it."

"I'll be home in ten minutes." He slid the phone into his pocket, started toward his car.

"Is everything okay?" Lauren kept pace beside him, her words filled with worry.

"I'm not sure. My son is having an allergic reaction to something. I've got to get home to make sure he's okay and to convince him to be a little more honest about what he's had to eat."

"Why don't I come with you? Once you get things settled, we can go over the list of his allergens. That way I can get started on the menu right away."

Surprised, Seth paused with his hand on the car door, turning to face Lauren. "And get our business over with more quickly?"

She shrugged, a thick dark curl sliding over her shoulder and resting at the V of her dress. "The sooner we do, the sooner I can get started on my vacation."

"I think maybe I should be insulted."

"It's nothing personal." And neither was their business agreement. She didn't have to add the rest for Seth to hear it.

"I get that."

"If you'd rather we take care of things by e-mail and phone, that's fine."

"Now works. If you don't think you'll be missed."

"I'll be missed, but I'll give Dee a call on her cell phone to let her know what's going on."

"Then let's go." He rounded the car, pulled open the passenger side door, inhaling a whiff of subtle perfume as Lauren slid in.

Perfume. Understated elegance. Dark wild curls. Confidence. Not the Lauren he'd dated for five years.

The changes should have made her a stranger. They didn't. And as Seth started the engine and drove toward home, he couldn't help thinking that having her in his car, having her beside him felt good. Even right.

And that was something he shouldn't be thinking at all.

THREE

Lauren needed to learn how to keep her mouth shut. That much was obvious. First, she'd offered to take part in Steff's auction. Now, she'd invited herself to Seth's house. What was it going to be next? Offering to cook an extra week of meals for free?

Just the thought of spending more time with Seth and his son made her cringe.

She needed to keep as much distance between herself and Seth as possible because, no matter how much she might want to claim otherwise, he still affected her. His smile could still make her pulse accelerate and her world tilt; looking into his eyes could still make her melt.

Fortunately, her head knew enough to keep her heart in check. Seth had the same charming personality that had attracted her when she'd been a shy teenager, but she wasn't a teenager anymore. She was a woman with a career, friends, a social life. Or as much of one as she wanted.

"This is it." Seth pulled into the driveway of a two-story farmhouse.

This was where he lived?

An old farmhouse?

He pushed open the door, and Lauren stepped inside. She'd been expecting something modern and sleek, but the dimly lit foyer had turn-of-the-century charm—wide planked floors, crown molding, a chandelier that looked original to the house, an atmosphere that whispered "home."

Seth pulled the door shut and started up the steps, calling out as he went, the deep timbre of his voice tinged with worry. "Reese? Jake?"

"We're in Jake's room." The feminine voice had to belong to the babysitter. A college student? A relative?

Lauren moved down the length of the foyer, her gaze lingering on the framed photos that hung on the wall. Most were family portraits. First Seth and a stunning blond dressed in wedding finery and smiling into each other's eyes. Then Seth standing behind the woman, his hand on her shoulder, his gaze on the tiny infant she held. Two more family photos followed, the infant older in each, but still small and fragile looking. The next photos were of Seth and his son, the boy more robust and sturdy, his mother absent.

"I probably need to get more interesting art for that wall." Seth spoke as he descended the stairs, his voice different than it had been years ago. Deeper, rougher, but still with an edge of polish and charm Lauren knew most women would find hard to resist.

Good thing she wasn't most women. "Why? Family photos are the best kind of artwork."

"They make my son happy, anyway. He loves looking at them and trying to remember the day they were taken."

Which seemed to imply that they didn't make Seth happy. Lauren had heard rumors about his marriage, the difficulties he and his wife had had. Whether or not those rumors were true didn't make any difference to her. He'd made his choice. She might not have been happy at the time, but in the end it had been for the best. "Your son is adorable and your wife was beautiful. I was sorry to hear of your loss."

"Thank you." The words were simple, his gaze lingering for just a moment on the wedding photo before he turned his attention back to her. "Jake and Reese will be down in a minute."

"Did he tell you what he'd eaten?"

"A cupcake a friend at school gave him."

"Store-bought?"

"No. Homemade."

"Even worse."

"So I've told him a thousand or so times. Come on in the kitchen, and I'll give you the list of the food Jake is allergic to." He led her down the hall and into a brightly lit kitchen. Granite countertops, white cabinets and stainless steel appliances made for an updated space without distracting from the beauty of the antique wood floor and trim. It was the kind of kitchen Lauren loved to work in, the kind she would have had if she lived in her own home rather than a rental.

"Here you go." Seth handed her a laminated sheet of paper. Tree nuts. Peanuts. Milk. Gluten. "His diet is quite limited."

"I'm hoping you can change that."

"I can give you ideas for interesting meals. A lot of kid-friendly stuff that uses other ingredients, but tastes almost the same as what his peers are eating." The sooner the better. Being in Seth's house, seeing the pictures of his wife and son only made her more anxious to fulfill her obligation and put the entire experience behind her.

"That's exactly what I'm looking for. This year has been tough for Jake. He wants to fit in with the other kids, but no matter where he goes or what he's doing, food is an issue."

Before Lauren could respond, a young boy rushed into the room, his red-gold hair mussed, pink blotches marring his neck and arms. "Hey, Dad…" He saw Lauren and skidded to a stop, his cheeks going scarlet. "Oh. Hi. You must be the cook."

"That's right. And you must be Jacob."

"And since we're all introducing ourselves, I'm Reese." A young blond stepped into the room, her makeup perfect, her hair artfully tousled. The babysitter? If so, she wasn't the kind of babysitter Lauren remembered from her own youth.

"I'm Lauren Owens."

"Good to meet you." Reese smiled and moved up beside Seth, her posture staking a claim Lauren wasn't sure she had a right to.

Not that the validity of her claim mattered. Seth's dating life had nothing to do with Lauren.

"Dad said you're going to make some cool food for me to bring to school."

"I *said* Lauren was going to teach us how to cook some more interesting meals. I didn't say anything about her making food for you to bring to school."

"Oh." Jake's cheeks turned a shade darker, his slumped shoulders and obvious embarrassment tugging at Lauren's heart. She knew exactly how he felt. Her own childhood had seemed like one big blur of timidity and embarrassment.

"Your dad paid for a week's worth of meals. That includes lunches, so I'll definitely be making you some things to take to school."

"Cool. Can you make cookies without gluten or nuts?"

"Sure."

"How about brownies?"

"Yep."

"Can you—"

"Jake." Seth's quiet reprimand was enough to heat Jake's cheeks again.

Poor kid. "I've got a lot of ideas, but I want to get them all together before we discuss them more."

"When will that be?"

"Not tonight." Seth put a hand on his son's shoulder. "I've got to take Lauren home. Do you mind staying for a little longer, Reese?"

"Not at all." The perky peppiness of the words reminded Lauren of the cheerleaders she'd known in high school.

"She doesn't have to stay, Dad. I'll be fine by myself for a while."

"You're ten. Not twenty, Jake. And I'm not ready to leave you home alone yet."

"I'll call Dee and have her come pick me up."

"There's no need for that. Reese is happy to stay, and I'm happy to give you a ride. You be good, kid." Seth ruffled his son's hair and started toward the kitchen door.

Lauren could argue or follow.

She met Reese's gaze, saw the younger woman's curiosity and decided to argue *after* she followed Seth out of the room.

Outside, the night had grown silent and still, the air

cool with late summer and darkness. Overhead, the moon shone bright in a clear star-dappled sky. It was the perfect night for long walks and hand-holding, for quiet conversation and whispered promises. A perfect night for romance if a person was into that sort of thing.

Lauren definitely wasn't. A few dates. A few dinners. A few phone conversations. She didn't let things go further than that. She didn't want them to. Dating was fine. Making plans, sharing dreams, those were other things entirely.

"I suppose you're going to insist on calling Dee." Seth spoke quietly as Lauren moved toward the edge of the porch.

"It makes more sense than having you take me to her place."

"Maybe, but I don't think Dee will appreciate you cutting into her evening. Besides, I owe you one."

"You've paid for the services I'm providing, Seth. You don't owe me anything."

"I haven't paid yet."

"You still don't owe me anything."

"No, but if I were anyone else, you'd take the ride and let Dee enjoy her evening."

"Maybe."

"Maybe?"

"Probably."

"So, let me give you a ride." He grinned, the fine lines near the corners of his eyes deepening and wiping away whatever vestiges of the boy she'd known remained. No more gangly teenager or broad-shouldered young man. Seth was hard edges and muscle hidden beneath charming wrappings.

Someone worth avoiding.

Which was why she should get out her phone and call Dee.

Of course she wouldn't because that would mean letting Seth know just how desperate she was to keep her distance. "All right. As long as it's no trouble."

"None at all." His fingers brushed against her lower back as he urged her down the steps and toward the car.

Lauren took a quick step away, uncomfortable with the warmth that spread through her at his touch. She would *not* react to Seth.

"You don't have to run away, Lola. I don't bite."

"I'm not running. And I told you not to call me that."

"Old habit." He opened the passenger side door, a smile playing at the corners of his mouth. "I'll try to break it."

"Please do."

He chuckled, the sound vibrating in the air and tickling against her ear as she slid into the car. Riding to Dee's house with Seth was one more bad decision piled on top of several others. It was past time to stop making them. Unfortunately, she seemed to be on a roll. After months of avoiding men and relationships she was sitting in a car with the one man she would have been happy to never see again. The only man she'd ever truly loved. The man who'd shown her just how fickle love could be.

"You're quiet." Seth's voice was soft silk and dark chocolate. The kind of decadence that could get a woman into trouble if she let it.

"Just thinking."

"About?"

You. "Jake. He reminds me a little of myself when I was his age."

"It's funny you should say that. I've often thought that he could be…" He shrugged. "He reminds me of you, too. A little shy. A little cautious."

"A little boring?"

"You were never boring."

But she hadn't been interesting enough to keep his attention. "I'm sure Jake isn't, either. Does he play sports?"

"Just baseball. His size has been an issue. He's a lot smaller than other boys his age."

"But he has other activities he enjoys?"

"Music. Video games. Playing with his friends. Normal ten-year-old stuff."

They were on safer conversational ground, and Lauren planned to stay there. "He seems like a good kid."

"He is. There isn't a day that goes by that I don't think of how blessed I am to have him."

A child *was* a blessing. One that Lauren had longed for when she'd been dreaming of marriage. Nowadays, she tried not to think about what her life was missing, concentrating instead on what she had.

"You really are blessed, Seth." Her throat was tight around the words, and she cleared it. Maybe this conversation wasn't as safe as she'd thought it. "I'd better call Dee."

A quick phone call provided Dee with minimum information and probably had her anxious to hear the details. Lauren would fill her in later. For now, she just wanted to get back to Dee's guesthouse and away from Seth.

"Is she okay with you skipping out on her?"

"Of course. Dee is always fine on her own."

"I take it she still loves to party?"

"She loves to be around people. That's always been her

gift. Take the next left. Dee's house is just a few miles from here."

"You seem like you've gotten more comfortable with crowds, too."

"Eleven years is plenty of time to get comfortable with just about anything." And that was all she was going to say on the subject. Seth didn't need to know how hard that first year without him had been, or how she'd realized that she'd relied on him too much. "Why don't you tell me a little about what Jake enjoys eating?"

Seth shot a look in her direction, but didn't comment on her quick change in subject. "The kind of stuff any kid loves—pizza, hamburgers, chicken. Sweets. At least those are the things he'd like to eat."

"I can make some variations that he'll enjoy."

"Sounds good. Where to now?"

"Turn right. Dee's house is there. The first one on the left."

Seth pulled into the driveway.

Finally.

Lauren shoved the car door open and hopped out. "Thanks for the ride, Seth. I'll be in touch."

She started toward the house, wobbling a little in her heels as she moved from the paved driveway to a stone path that led to the backyard.

"You're not going inside?" Seth stepped up beside her.

"No. Dee has a guesthouse out back. I'm staying there."

"I'll walk you around."

"There's no need."

"Of course there is."

"Seth—"

"A body was found buried under the sidewalk at the college a week ago, Lauren. A little caution makes sense."

"Whatever happened to that poor girl happened a long time ago. I don't think I need to worry about it."

"No? If she was murdered, a killer is walking free. I think that's something we all need to be concerned about."

Lauren wasn't sure she agreed, but Seth's words still made her shiver. "*If* she was murdered. It's possible she died of natural causes or that she fell into the construction area and died from her injuries."

"And somehow got buried beneath enough dirt that the crew pouring the sidewalk didn't see her? That seems highly unlikely."

"Maybe so, but I doubt a murderer would be hanging around town waiting for his crime to be discovered. Even if he is still around, I doubt he'll be coming after anyone else."

"Maybe he already has. Maybe there are other victims. We don't know and, until we do, I think it's best if we all be careful."

That was definitely not a thought Lauren wanted to dwell on as she continued toward the edge of Dee's property and the small carriage house that stood there.

An outside light glowed above the bright red door, lighting the cement stoop and the thick bushes that stood on either side of it. Lauren fumbled for her keys, pulled them out of the sequined handbag she carried and unlocked the door, reaching in to flick on the living room light before she turned to say goodbye to Seth. "Thanks for the ride. And the walk."

"Thanks for helping me with my son." His hair looked deeper red in the light, his eyes dark and unreadable. The years showed in the creases near his mouth, the fine lines near the corners of his eyes. Each spoke of time passing and of the life he'd lived in the time since they'd last seen each other. As much as she wanted to believe she didn't care, Lauren couldn't stop the emotion that clogged her throat and made speaking difficult.

She swallowed, forcing back all the things she knew she shouldn't be feeling. "It won't take me long to create the menus. I'll contact you as soon as I'm finished."

"I'm looking forward to it." He smiled and her heart responded even as her head shouted that she was a fool.

"Good night." She stepped inside and closed the door, shutting out Seth's smile and the uncomfortable emotions it evoked.

But she couldn't deny that she'd felt them, that somehow, despite all that had happened, she responded to Seth in a way she hadn't responded to many other men. To *any other men.*

The truth didn't sit well with her, and she paced across the small living room, frustration making her want to get in the car and drive back to Savannah and the life she'd created there. Sure, she'd needed this vacation, but she didn't need to spend time with Seth and his sweet, shy son.

"They're clients. Just like any other client you've worked for." She muttered the words as she stepped into her bedroom and grabbed her Bible from the suitcase she'd left on the bed.

Clients. She could say the word a hundred times, and it wouldn't make things any less complicated than they were.

Lauren opened French doors that led out onto a small patio. Honeysuckle-scented air drifted into the room, the sweet smell reminding her of carefree childhood summers.

Frogs called to one another, their deep song mournful and lonely. Or maybe it was Lauren who was both those things.

She flicked on the outside light, determined not to be melancholy. This was her vacation, and she wasn't going to spend it thinking about past heartaches.

Moonlight played over the trees that edged Dee's property, casting deep shadows across the lawn. It should have been beautiful. It was beautiful. There was something else there, though. A darkness that seemed more than night and shadow. A shape that wasn't quite the same as those around it.

Lauren shook away the thought.

Obviously, Seth's talk of bodies and murder had her imagination working overtime. Reading her daily Bible study would ground her. At least Lauren hoped it would. She opened the worn leather cover and tried to immerse herself in her reading, but the more she tried, the more conscious she became of the strange shape at the corner edge of the yard.

"It's nothing." She spoke loudly, hoping the sound would chase away the warning that hummed along her nerves. Her voice broke through the mournful call of frogs and soft drone of insects, and the night creatures fell silent as if waiting for her to continue.

She didn't, but in the sudden stillness new sounds emerged, the crackle of dry leaves, the snap of a branch. Then silence so deep it felt as if the world were holding its breath, waiting for whatever lurked in the shadows to make its move.

Lauren stood, clutching her Bible in her hand and backing toward the door. "Hello? Is someone there?"

She didn't expect an answer, and she didn't get one,

though she thought she heard the rasp of someone's breath, felt the weight of someone's gaze.

One step at a time, she eased toward the door afraid to turn her back on the darkness and whatever hid there. It wasn't until she was inside, the doors locked and lights blazing, that she realized just how silly she was being. Despite what Seth had said, there was nothing to be afraid of. She knew that, she'd just forgotten it for a minute.

Still, she felt compelled to pull the drapes across the French doors and check the windows to make sure they were locked.

She'd just stepped back into the living room when a firm knock sounded on the door. She jumped, her heart slamming against her ribs, her gaze flying to the mantel clock. Eleven o'clock seemed an odd time for a visitor. She grabbed the fireplace poker, striding toward the door with more confidence than she felt and praying that whomever was out there was someone she'd be happy to see.

FOUR

"Who's there?" To Lauren's disgust, her voice wobbled on the last word.

"Me." Dee knocked again. "Who were you expecting? Jack the Ripper?"

Lauren pulled the door open, stepping aside to let her sister in. "I don't know, but I wasn't expecting *you*. What are you doing back so early?"

"Early? I'm not seventeen anymore, sis. This is late."

"Right. You came to check up on me."

"Okay. So I came back to see what was going on. Sue me."

"That would require a lawyer, and I've had about all I can take of lawyers for one evening."

"I'd sympathize, but you did it to yourself, offering to meet Seth's son tonight."

"It seemed like the right thing to do at the time."

"Did it?" Dee settled down into an overstuffed chair. "To me it seemed crazy."

Lauren laughed and settled down on the sofa. "Why don't you try being blunt next time?"

"I call it like I see it. So? Tell me."

"Tell you what?"

"What happened."

"Nothing happened. I went to Seth's house, met his son, looked at the list of Jake's allergens, came back here."

"Way to cut out all the details, sis."

"Those *are* the details."

"You and Seth didn't say one word to each other on the ride from the inn to his house? Not one word from his house here? Come on, Laur, I know there's more to the story than you're telling."

"Because you *want* there to be more. There isn't though. Just boring conversation between two people who used to know each other." Sure there'd been a hint of attraction still there, but that wasn't something Dee needed to know, and it wasn't something Lauren planned to share.

Or dwell on.

Seth was the last person she wanted to spend time thinking about.

"Too bad. I was hoping for some juicy tidbits to share with the girls." She smirked and ran a hand over her hair. "Anyway, nosiness isn't the only thing that brought me back here. Steff asked when we'd be ready to launch the Magnolia Falls: Where Are They Now Web site. I wanted to check with you on that before Jennifer and I gave her an answer."

"Any time Jen is ready." The owner of a nursery school in Magnolia Falls, Jen Pappas had always been great with computers, and Lauren had enlisted her help with designing the Web site.

"Monday? That'll give you two days to clean out your e-mail in-box before you're inundated with alumni news."

"Inundated? I'm just hoping we'll get back in touch with a few people we went to school with." Several of those people hadn't returned for their ten-year reunion. In itself, that wasn't worrisome. The fact that a body had been found on campus was. Could it be one of the people she'd gone to school with? Shared laughter, tears and friendship with? Lauren prayed not.

"Be prepared anyway. Steff sent a letter out to alumni letting them know about the site."

"I got it the other day. Of course, receiving notice about the Web site doesn't mean participating in it. There will be plenty of people who won't bother signing the guest book or filling out the information questionnaire."

"True. We'll see what happens Monday. Jennifer and I have got things set up so that guest book entries have to be approved before they're seen on the site. That way we'll have a chance to screen things before they're out for public view. We decided that could be your job for now. When you get tired of doing it, one of the rest of us will take over."

One of the rest of them included Dee, Steff, Cassie, Jennifer or Kate. Close friends in college, they'd made it a point to stay close in the years since. "I suppose you all voted on this while I was away from the table."

"Yep. We figured you were on vacation and had more time than the rest of us."

"You figured that since I left the fund-raiser early you could foist the job off on me."

"That, too."

Lauren laughed and tossed a throw pillow at her sister.

Dee caught it and stood, stretching her lean frame, the vivid blue of her dress striking against fair skin. Thirty-two and still single. With her looks and personality, Lauren had thought her sister would have married long ago.

Lauren had thought *she* would have married long ago, too.

Yet here they both were single and unattached.

And happy about it?

For her part, yes. She wasn't so sure about her sister.

"What?" Dee brushed a hand across her mouth. "Do I have something on my face?"

"No, I was just thinking that you should have gone to the fund-raiser with some handsome Prince Charming. Not with me."

"Please. As if there is such a thing." She started toward the front door. "I'm going to head back to the house. Want to come up and watch a movie?"

"No, I think I'll unpack and read for a while."

"Suit yourself. I'll see you tomorrow." She stepped outside and Lauren followed, hovering in the doorway as Dee walked toward the house, the same fear that had shivered along her spine before Dee arrived lodging in her throat once again as she watched her sister move toward the darkness at the edge of the house.

"Are you going in the back door?"

Dee turned to face Lauren again. "No."

"I'll walk around front with you."

"Why?"

Because she was worried about a murderer who might not even exist. "It's dark."

"Lauren, I come home after dark six nights out of seven."

"I know, but…" But what? "Seth was saying—"

"I *knew* you discussed more than his son's food allergies."

"He was saying that the remains found beneath the sidewalk might belong to someone who had been murdered."

"And? We've discussed that possibility a hundred times."

"And he mentioned the fact that a murderer may be wandering around Magnolia Falls."

Dee laughed. "You still haven't outgrown your penchant for worry, have you? But there's no need for it in this instance. First of all, we're not in Magnolia Falls. Secondly, if there is a murderer lurking around somewhere, he's had plenty of opportunity to kill again. Since the police haven't found bodies spread across town, I think I'm safe."

Lauren's cheeks heated at her sister's words.

Dee was right of course. Of the two, Lauren had always been the cautious one. The one prone to worry and wondering. Imagining worst-case scenarios. Monsters in closets. "Okay, so I'm worried, but maybe Seth is right. Maybe we all should be a little more cautious until the police find out what happened to the poor woman they found."

"Look, if it'll make you feel better, I'll go in the back door."

"It will."

Dee rolled her eyes, but nodded. "Fine. You stand and watch until I get inside. Not that either of us will be much good if a murderer really is out here. What do either of us know about self-defense?"

Not much, but Lauren decided not to think about that as she watched Dee make her way across the yard and into the house. Thinking about it would only make her worry, and worry was something she had too much practice at.

As soon as the back door closed, Lauren shut and locked the carriage house door, barring it against the darkness on the other side. Silly, she knew. But necessary. She checked the windows, the French doors, pulled the curtains and shades. Surveyed the cozy living room and kitchen area. Everything closed up tight.

Perfect. Now she could do her Bible study, relax a little, maybe log on to her computer and start planning Jake's meals. A nice cup of tea would be good. Maybe one of the scones she'd made that morning and brought with her on the trip.

Lauren grabbed both, then settled onto the love seat.

"Love is patient. Love is kind."

First Corinthians Thirteen?

Today was definitely not a good day to be reading about love. Maybe she'd skip a day ahead in her Bible study. She tried to focus on the next chapter, but her mind spun back to a time when love had seemed not just possible, but very, very real.

"What's wrong, Lola?" Seth cupped her face in his hands, his eyes the green of spring and of hope.

"You're leaving for college in a week. I'm going to miss you."

"I won't be that far away." He smiled, his fingers trailing from her jaw to her neck, amusement dancing in his eyes. "Just an hour's drive."

"Until I get my license and a car, it may as well be twenty hours away."

"I'll come home every weekend."

"You say that now." She and Seth had been going together for two years. He kept telling her that his leaving wouldn't change that, but she didn't believe him. There would be plenty of girls at the small college he'd chosen to attend. Plenty of girls who were probably more outgoing, more exciting than Lauren.

"And I mean it." Amusement was replaced by fire, his eyes glowing with sincerity. "I love you, Lola. How could I ever stay away from you for more than a few days?"

His words melted the ice in her chest, and she threw her arms around his broad, firm shoulders. "I love you, too, Seth."

Love.

Right.

Lauren shook her head, trying to dislodge the memories and the sadness that went with them. All these years after Seth had broken her heart and the memories still had the ability to choke her up. That said something about her, and Lauren was afraid it wasn't anything flattering.

Dreams. Hopes. Love.

They were part of the past and she really, really needed to leave them there.

She stood and paced across the floor. Of all the people that could have won her chef services, it seemed almost inconceivable that Seth was the top bidder.

"A few hundred people at the fund-raiser, and it had to be my old boyfriend who decided to make the highest bid. I guess you've got a reason, Lord, but I sure can't figure out what it might be."

Something scraped against the window above the kitchen sink and Lauren jumped, turning toward the sound, all thoughts of Seth, the past and God's plan fleeing.

The sound came again. This time more of a knock than a scrape, and Lauren was sure someone was outside, pressing against the glass.

Her heart slammed in her chest as she turned off the living room light and stepped into the kitchen. *Pull up the shade, Lauren. Look outside, you'll see that no one is there.*

Or maybe she'd see that someone *was* there.

Maybe she should call Dee and have her look out the

upstairs window. See if she could spot anyone lurking near the carriage house. Or maybe she should just pull back the shade and see for herself. After all, someone standing on the other side of the glass couldn't hurt her.

She grabbed the phone, held it in a sweaty hand as she eased the shade back from the window and stared into…nothing. No face with slitted, evil eyes. No ski-masked Peeping Tom. Just darkness. She leaned toward the glass, peering into the area behind the carriage house. Something had knocked against the glass. That hadn't been her imagination. A light by the French doors illuminated the backyard, and Lauren turned it on, then searched the lit area.

If someone had been there he was long gone.

As she watched a breeze ruffled the trees that lined the property and the bushes that abutted the back of the carriage house scraped against the siding. There. The sound she'd heard. Explained. So why was her pulse still racing, and what had she heard bumping against the glass? A branch? A stick? Nothing? The silence seemed almost eerie, the dark shadows that edged the property sinister. But then, compared to the well-lit, busy street she lived on in Savannah, anything would seem silent and dark.

Lauren let the shade drop back into place, but left the outside light on. She was pretty sure nothing but her imagination was skulking in the darkness, but keeping the yard lit seemed like a good idea. So did focusing on something other than bodies hidden for ten years; murderers. Seth. The best way to get him out of her mind was to get him out of her life, and that meant fulfilling her obligation.

She pulled her laptop out of its case, moved her ginger tea and scone to the small kitchen table and booted up the computer. A few minutes later, she was scrolling through nut-free, gluten-free recipes. A day or two and she'd have the menu planned, then it would just be a matter of going to Seth's house and cooking the meals. It was the same thing she'd done hundreds of times before with dozens of clients. This time felt different, but she'd ignore that and concentrate on doing what she did best—creating fun, exciting meals for a kid whose diet was limited by allergies. When she was done she'd move on to the next client and put Seth and his son behind her.

She hoped. Though something told her there was going to be more to this job than cooking food and more to her relationship with Seth and Jake than business. What that might be she didn't know. She could only pray that the end result would be something positive.

FIVE

The menus were done. Breakfast, lunch and dinner for seven days. Twenty-one meals. Fourteen snacks. Plenty of things a ten-year-old might enjoy. All Lauren had to do was call Seth and set up a day to cook the meals.

And she would.

Eventually.

For now, she was going to enjoy Sunday morning and not worry about seeing Seth again.

She pulled on a pale lavender sweater, ran her fingers through nearly dry curls and dusted on translucent powder. A little lip gloss, her purse and she was ready to go to church. Too bad she didn't know where the nearest one was. Dee might, but Lauren doubted it. Her sister wasn't much for attending church. She wasn't much for religion, God, faith, but today was a new day. Maybe Dee would come along. It wouldn't hurt to ask.

"You're up early." Dee swung open the front door to her house, her deeply shadowed eyes taking in Lauren's appearance. "And ready to go. Should I guess where?"

"Church. Any suggestions?"

"Magnolia Christian."

"I was thinking a little closer to your place."

"Sorry. I'm sure there are a dozen within a mile of here, but I don't know them."

"It's okay. I'll head toward Magnolia Falls. If I don't see a church before I reach Main Street, I'll go to Magnolia Christian. Want to come?"

"It's tempting, but I'm not dressed." Dee smiled, but it was more gritted teeth than amusement.

"I can wait."

"Sorry, sis. I'm not up for it this morning. Maybe next week." Which meant maybe never.

Lauren bit back a sigh and conceded. Insisting would only cause an argument and hurt feelings. "I guess I'll see you when I get back."

"Or we could meet at the Half Joe around one. Have some coffee and something decadent. I can call the girls and see if anyone wants to join us."

"That's something I can definitely agree to."

"See you then."

Lauren nodded and started toward her car. A sixty-seven Mustang with gleaming yellow paint, it was her most daring purchase, something flashy and striking. Something un-Lauren-like.

Which had been the whole point.

Just once Lauren had wanted to be daring and different, edgy and fun. Maybe she'd achieved it, but there'd been no one around to tell her so. Just an empty Savannah apartment and a few carpenter ants that were trying to make their home in the walls.

A few miles outside of Magnolia Falls, Lauren spotted a small, white church set on a hill and thought about stopping, but it had been years since she'd attended Magnolia Christian Church, and she kept driving, winding her way along a rural road and into town.

Main Street was Sunday-morning quiet, the college campus barely awake. To the left, Magnolia Christian Church rose tall and handsome in the late-summer sun, the stone facade warm gray and inviting. There were so many memories here, so many good times and some that weren't so good.

"Lauren!" Cassie Winters hurried across the parking lot, her hair glossy fire, her eyes sparkling green. "I was hoping you'd be here today. I'm so glad you came!"

"I thought about finding a church closer to Dee's place, but Magnolia Christian just kind of called to me."

"I'm glad. After the late night, I wasn't sure any of the gang would be here." Cassie linked an arm through Lauren's and tugged her toward the church, her bouncy peppiness making Lauren feel almost sluggish in comparison.

"How late did you all leave?"

"After midnight. Things went well. Steff was pleased."

"I'm glad. Things have been stressful for her lately."

"Stressful, but good, too. I'm hoping she and Trevor will be here today. They're so cute together."

"Cute? Don't tell her that."

"I wouldn't dare."

Lauren laughed, the sound choking off as she caught sight of someone she hadn't even imagined she'd see there. Tall. Golden-red hair. Green eyes.

As if he felt the weight of her gaze, Seth turned his head, his vivid eyes meeting hers. A quick, warm smile lit his face before he turned away. Lauren's heart jumped, her pulse sped, and she silently called herself every kind of fool in the world.

"He's still got it, doesn't he?" Cassie's amusement was obvious.

"Who has what?"

"As if you don't know who I'm talking about. Mr. Tall, strawberry blond, handsome and completely charming."

"Strawberry blond, tall and handsome, yes. Charming? That's up for debate."

"Hardly. Seth epitomizes Southern gallantry."

"And you know this because…?"

"We've been attending the same church for a couple of years."

"And you never thought to mention this to me?"

"Why would I? You guys were an item eons ago, and I don't think you've mentioned his name once since you broke up. Far be it from me to be the one to bring him up."

Lauren had avoided any discussion of Seth, his marriage, his son, his wife's death, but it would have been nice to know he attended Magnolia Christian. If she had, she would have stopped at the little, white church on the hill. "Maybe coming today wasn't such a good idea."

Cassie raised an eyebrow. "Why? Because you wanted to avoid seeing Seth? That would seem like a wasted effort seeing as how you're cooking meals for him and his son."

"Don't remind me."

They were almost at the church doors, and Cassie stopped, turning to face Lauren. "Is it really that upsetting for you?"

"No, of course not. It's just uncomfortable."

"Uncomfortable is a pair of too-tight shoes, or vinyl car

seats on a hot summer day. Cooking dinner for a man who broke your heart is another thing altogether." Cassie's normally cheerful expression had turned serious, her eyes searching Lauren's face.

"I'll handle it."

"There's no doubt in my mind that you will. Just be careful. Seth isn't the same person he was when you two were dating. His focus is on his son, and he's a great dad. That's a pretty attractive quality. I'd hate to see you pulled into something that might not work out. I don't want your heart to be broken again."

"I'd have to fall for him to have my heart broken, and there is no way in this world I'd ever fall for Seth again."

"Maybe not, but be careful anyway." Cassie's somber expression eased, and she grabbed Lauren's hand. "Let's head in. Hey, maybe we can go to the Half Joe after church. Grab a cup of coffee and something sweet and gooey."

"Dee suggested the same thing."

"Which just proves what a smart lady your sister is."

Lauren laughed, her heels clicking on tile flooring as she walked into the church. It felt good to be here again. The buzz and hum of college students and Magnolia Falls residents, the echoes of laughter and conversation brought back memories of a time that had been much simpler. Sure there'd been stress in college—exams, the hurry of trying to finish her degree in three years rather than four, the worry about her relationship with Seth—but overall it had been fun, her dreams and hopes intact, her friends sure and true and steady. They still were. It was her dreams that had flown, her hopes that had to be readjusted. Marriage, a house in town, a white picket fence and cookies baking in the oven while children played in the yard. That's what she'd wanted. Maybe she'd even expected it. What she'd gotten was a whole lot different.

Which wasn't necessarily a bad thing. Years after the fact, she could finally acknowledge what she hadn't been able to when Seth had broken up with her—marriage to him would have been a slow death. He'd been too confident and driven to have patience with Lauren's timid emergence, her cautious entrance into the world.

She slid into the back pew next to Cassie and did her best to push thoughts of Seth out of her mind. She was here to worship and to learn, not to think about things that had never been part of God's plan for her life.

As the pastor rose to give the morning announcements a young boy scooted into the pew next to Lauren. She glanced over, her smile freezing in place as she caught sight of Seth's son. If he noticed who he was sitting with, he didn't acknowledge it, just stared straight ahead, his checks fire-engine red, the tips of his ears bright pink.

Seconds later, Seth slid in next to him, offering Lauren a quick glance and a half smile that didn't reach his eyes. Something was going on between father and son, but it wasn't Lauren's business.

She turned her attention back to the pastor, listening to the list of prayer requests and announcements and trying her best to ignore the redheaded boy beside her. That should have been easy enough. He was just a kid after all. Ten years old and gangly, as well. Freckled and pale when his cheeks weren't flushed with embarrassment.

Just a kid.

Just *Seth's* kid.

And somehow that made him impossible to ignore.

The prelude to the first hymn began, and Lauren reached for the hymnal, her hand bumping Jake's as he reached for the same one.

"Sorry, ma'am." He whispered the apology as he grabbed another book, his cheeks going scarlet again.

Poor kid.

"No problem. It's Jake, right?" She spoke close to his ear, and was surprised by a quick grin that reminded her so much of Seth it speared her heart.

"Right. And you're Miss Lauren. Dad said we shouldn't sit by you, but I didn't want to walk all the way to the front with everyone watching."

"Understandable."

"That's what I thought." His eyes were wide and green, his cheeks and nose splattered with freckles. He'd be a heartbreaker one day. Right now, he was just a little boy who buried his nose in the hymnal and seemed content to mumble rather than sing the words.

Lauren lifted her gaze, met Seth's searching look. Whatever he was thinking was hidden by too many years of not knowing one another, and she turned away, determined not to glance in his direction again.

Seth should be paying attention to Pastor Rogers's sermon, but his focus kept shifting. He could blame it on a late night or a stressful week, but Seth believed in calling things the way they were. He was distracted. Plain and simple. Not by his upset ten-year-old, not even by his own frustration with Jake's timid nature. Not by late nights and busy days. No, he was distracted by Lauren. Her black skirt and pale purple sweater were a perfect foil for dark hair and porcelain skin. She hadn't worn makeup, and her understated beauty reminded him of the way she'd looked the day they'd met. Sweet. Fragile. Needy. Nothing like the strong, confident woman of the previous night.

She scratched notes in a small leather journal as the pastor spoke. That, too, reminded Seth of the past. Lauren's meticulous and careful nature had appealed to him when they'd met. Eventually, he'd come to resent those things. Young, brash, eager for life and adventure, he'd been sure that he needed to be with someone more like him. Someone ready to take the bull by the horn. Someone not afraid to take chances. He'd broken up with Lauren before he transferred to law school, breaking the promises he'd made while he was at it.

Did he regret it?

That was a question he'd never been able to answer. Not when his actions had given him Jake. But he did regret hurting Lauren. When he'd returned to Magnolia College to apologize, he'd gotten his first glimpse of the woman she'd one day become and had felt the first stirring of something beyond the protective, sheltering love he'd had for her.

Jake shifted in the pew, pulling Seth's thoughts back to the present. He leaned close, whispering in his son's ear. "You sure you don't want to go to Sunday school?"

"And watch everyone eat Brandon's birthday cupcakes? No way."

He spoke loudly enough that several people glanced in their direction.

"Keep it down, buddy."

"Sorry." Jake's cheeks turned tomato-red, and he slumped in his seat looking about as dejected as a ten-year-old could.

Lauren leaned toward him, whispering something in his ear that made him nod.

What had she said? Something that erased the dejection from Jake's face, that was for sure.

Pastor Rogers concluded his sermon with a prayer for God's purpose and will to be worked in the lives of each person in the congregation.

Seth added his own prayer—that God would help him be the kind of father Jake needed, that he wouldn't repeat his own parents' mistakes and cause a rift with his child that could never be healed. He didn't think he could bear having Jake out in the world as Ellen was, without family.

"Guess what, Dad." Jake turned to him as soon as the strains of the last hymn died out.

"What?"

"Lauren—"

"Miss Lauren."

"Miss Lauren said she's going to make brownies for me to bring to Sunday school next week."

"Brownies?" He met Lauren's eyes, smiling as heat crept up her cheeks. "Sans gluten? Is that possible?"

"Yes. And they'll be so good Jake's friends will be begging their mothers to make them for their birthdays." She smiled, but Seth knew it was for Jake's benefit. The look in her eyes was much cooler than her expression, her voice frosty despite the warmth of the words.

"Really?" Jake was nearly bouncing with excitement. "That would be great. Some of the guys think I'm weird because I can never eat the stuff they bring, and I want to show them that I'm the same as them."

"Of course you are. All ten-year-old boys are weird."

Jake's eyes widened, then, to Seth's surprise, he laughed. "Yeah, well I think all chefs are weird."

"Jake—"

"It's okay. If we're both weird we'll get along great." Lauren smiled down at Jake, and Seth decided not to reprimand his son further.

"When can you make the brownies?"

"I'll make them when I come over to cook your meals."

"Tomorrow?"

"Probably not. Your dad and I have to work out a time after he approves the menu."

"Oh. Okay."

"You've got the menus done already?" She worked quickly. Probably hoping to get the job done and Seth out of her life as soon as possible. Seth couldn't blame her for that.

"Yes. I'll e-mail them to you later today. You can call me once you've looked them over." Cool, professional, distant, her voice was everything it should be when speaking to a man she was doing business with. The thing was, there was a lot more than business between them, and for some reason he didn't want to name, Seth had the urge to prove it.

"Lola—" He wasn't sure what he wanted to say, what he could say that would break down the icy wall she'd erected, but Cassie Winters nudged at Lauren's back and interrupted, her tone crisp and clipped.

"Aren't we supposed to be meeting your sister at the Half Joe, *Lauren?*"

Even a dense man wouldn't have missed the emphasis on Lauren's name.

"Yes. We'd better get moving. I'll talk to you soon, Seth.

Bye, Jake." They hurried away before Seth could finish whatever he'd been about to say. It was probably for the best. There really was nothing *to* say. The past was just that and had nothing to do with the job Lauren was being paid to do or the reasons why Seth had hired her. He'd do well to keep that in mind. Somehow, though, he had a feeling that was going to be a lot more difficult than it should be.

SIX

The Half Joe had been a favorite hangout of Lauren and her friends during their college years. Cozy and filled with chairs and sofas, nooks and study corners, it was the perfect place to unwind. Even now, ten years after graduation, Lauren appreciated the relaxing ambience and comfortable decor.

Sunday afternoon brought plenty of business to the coffee shop, and it was filled with students bent over books and typing on laptops. True to her word, Dee had managed to contact the other girls, and she, Kate, Steff and Jennifer were all sipping coffee as Lauren and Cassie walked in.

"You couldn't wait for us, huh?" Cassie took the chair next to Kate, and Lauren eased down onto an overstuffed sofa occupied by Dee and Jennifer.

"We weren't sure you were actually coming. Jennifer said she saw the two of you talking to Seth and his son after church." Dee speared Lauren with the kind of look only an older sister could give. "She said you were sitting together during church."

"They were. I would have stopped to chat, but I didn't want to interrupt." Jennifer Pappas sipped her own coffee, then stood, her tall, thin frame encased in a navy dress, her dark hair pulled back in a neat chignon. "I don't know about you all, but I'm ready for one of those fancy éclairs they make here."

"An éclair sounds good. What do the rest of you want?" Lauren stood, desperate to move the conversation away from Seth and his son.

The rest of the ladies stood and moved toward the counter, their attention focused on the pastries displayed there. A few minutes later, they were all back in over-stuffed chairs and sofas, leaning in close and talking quietly about the success of the fund-raiser dinner.

This was more like it. Coffee. Sweets. Girl talk. The kind of easy Sunday afternoon that invited friendship and closeness.

Lauren should have known it wasn't going to last; that Dee wouldn't be able to let the subject of Seth drop.

"So, who sat with whom? Did you sit with Seth and his son, or did they decide to sit next to you?" Dee whispered the question in her ear, but the others heard, their conversation sputtering to a stop as each turned to look at Lauren. All eyes filled with curiosity and, unless Lauren missed her guess, worry.

"Seth's son sat next to Lauren. He's a nice kid. A little shy, but sweet and very respectful." Cassie spoke into the sudden silence, her peppy, upbeat tone a little too forced.

"I can't believe Seth let him." Dee ran a hand over her perfectly styled hair and shook her head. "You'd think he'd keep as far away from Lauren as possible after what he did to her."

"What he did happened over a decade ago, Dee. I think we're both over it by now, and I think you and I have had this conversation before. How about we change the subject before it gets boring?" Lauren kept her tone steady and firm, asserting herself as she hadn't been able to when she was younger.

Kate nodded, her long, brown hair sliding over her shoulders as she leaned toward Lauren. "I agree. What I'd love to know is when the Web site is going to be launched. It's exciting to think about reconnecting with old friends. Finding out if their lives went according to plans they made when they were young." Her words were wistful, her fingers tight around the coffee cup she held. Her dreams had died the same kind of death Lauren's had. But Kate's resulted in a child, a divorce and a return to Magnolia Falls.

"*When they were young?* Honey, I still *am* young." Cassie shoved strands of straight red hair behind her ear. "And I can tell you for sure, all those dreams I made in college have been fulfilled."

"I seem to recall a certain redheaded gymnast dreaming about Mr. Wonderful, a house, kids." Jennifer's dark eyes were filled with amusement.

"Like I said, I'm still young. There's plenty of time for all that."

Lauren laughed, settling back into her chair. "You're the most upbeat person I know, Cassie."

"Which is why you love me." Cassie grinned and took a bite out of the double chocolate muffin she'd purchased. "So? Have you decided on the Web site's launch date? I'm as excited about it as Kate."

"We'll be up and running tomorrow."

"I'll send out an e-mail to the alumni on our mailing list." The alumni relations director for Magnolia College, Steff was always quick to move forward with projects that could enhance the alumni association's bottom line. The launch of Magnolia Falls: Where Are They Now could very well do that.

"That sounds great, Steff. I'm just hoping some of the people who aren't on your mailing list will find us. It would be great to hear from some of our old friends."

"I'd love to catch up with Angela Heaton and Josie Skerritt. I can't believe it's been ten years since I've spoken to either of them." Jennifer frowned, and Lauren could imagine what she was thinking. Both Angela and Josie had been in the education program at Magnolia College, they'd both graduated the same year as Lauren.

They'd both fallen off the face of the earth.

"And Payton Bell. Remember how sweet she was?" Cassie brushed strands of hair from her cheek.

"Too sweet." Dee bit into an oversize chocolate chip cookie and frowned. "But that doesn't mean I want to imagine something bad happening to her."

"Then let's not." Steff brushed crumbs off her dark suit, her expression somber. "I talked to the police earlier today. The forensic expert they contacted has determined that the woman they found was in her late teens to early twenties. There's a good chance she'd recently given birth."

"Given birth?!" The chorus of voices drew the attention of a dozen or more Half Joe patrons, and Lauren leaned in toward her friends, her mind sick with possibilities.

"The baby wasn't buried with her, was it?"

"No. That's the thing. They don't know who she was, and they don't know what happened to the baby."

"I can't imagine—"

"Ladies, what a pleasure to see you all here." Cornell

Rutherford approached from across the room. Head of the English Department at Magnolia College, he'd taught several of Lauren's English classes when she attended school there, his staid, old-world manners sometimes more affected than real.

"Dr. Rutherford. It's good to see you." She started to stand, but he motioned her back down.

"Don't bother getting up, my dear. I'm just in for a cup of coffee and really can't chat. It seems the six of you are having a meeting of minds." His silver hair and tall, regal bearing gave him an air of old-time aristocracy, his suave, polished manners almost too perfect. Still, he was well-respected at the college and in the community, and he had a reputation as a kind, but strict professor.

"We're discussing the launch of the new Web site I told you about." Steff smiled at Cornell and he nodded.

"That's right. I'd forgotten you were getting that underway. How's it going?"

"We'll be online tomorrow. You should check it out. Maybe you can be the first to sign the guest book. Some of your former students would probably be interested to know that you're now head of the English department."

"I think I'll do that. Right now, though, I've really got to run." He moved away, his gait unhurried, his carriage straight.

"He gets more full of himself every year," Dee mumbled under her breath, and Steff's eyes widened.

"That's not a very nice thing to say."

"And he's not a very nice man."

"He's not unkind, either." Lauren stepped into the conversation.

"No, he's just arrogant and self-important." Dee finished

off the cookie she was eating and wiped crumbs from her dark jeans. "But most of the guys I know are that, so maybe it's an epidemic in today's world."

"You just haven't met the right guys. There are plenty of men of integrity out there." Steff's expression softened as she spoke.

"There's only one Trevor, Steff. The rest of the male population doesn't quite live up to the example he sets." Dee stood and stretched. "I think I'll head home. I've got a big marketing campaign I'm spearheading at work. There's no time like the present to get working on it."

"I think I'll head back, too." Lauren grabbed her purse and the remainder of her éclair. "I've got to e-mail the menu plan to Seth today. The sooner I can get this over with the happier I'll be."

"Let me know when you start getting guest book submissions, Lauren. I'm anxious to see if we hear from any of our missing alumni." Steff stood, too, and Lauren knew she wasn't anxious because she was hoping to recruit more financial donors.

No, she was anxious to know that her old college buddies were safe and happy and not newly discovered dead beneath the sidewalk outside of Kessler Library.

No one voiced the worry, but the thought seemed to hang in the air as Lauren and her friends left the Half Joe and started toward their cars.

The police might not have identified the remains that had been found during the remodeling of the library, but Lauren had the sinking feeling she'd known the person, that the remains belonged to someone she'd once studied with, laughed with, shared dreams and goals with.

Dead for ten years and never missed.

She shuddered and scrambled into the Mustang, yanking the door shut and locking it against the evil that might still lurk somewhere in Magnolia Falls.

"Get a grip, Lauren. Magnolia Falls is no different than it ever was." She mumbled the words as she pulled out onto Main Street, but she didn't quite believe her own words.

Magnolia Falls *was* different. A shadow hung over it now, a darkness that hadn't been there before. Her imagination. Yes. But something else, too. Something real and frightening. A body. Maybe a murder. *Probably* a murder. How else had the poor woman gotten under the sidewalk?

Lauren flicked on the radio, trying to drown out the sound of her own thoughts. It didn't work, and she circled around to the same idea she'd had when she'd first heard that someone had been buried beneath a layer of cement. Magnolia College wasn't a large school by most university standards. The tight-knit community that surrounded it was filled with people who knew each other. Could someone have disappeared a decade ago and their presence *not* be missed?

So maybe it wasn't a student or even a resident of Magnolia Falls. Maybe the woman who'd died was a vagrant, someone who'd been ill and died alone.

And been buried how?

She could think about it all day and not find an answer. It was a good thing she didn't have to. What had happened, how the woman had ended up under the sidewalk was for the police to find out.

Lauren turned off Main Street and headed out of town, the windows down, music playing over the radio. A few days, a week tops, and she'd be done with Seth and his son and ready to start her vacation. All she had to do was figure out what to do with her free time. Five or so empty days. No meals to plan. No menus. No client meetings or marathon cooking sessions. Just Lauren and the solitude of Dee's guesthouse, the silence of a day filled with nothing and nobody. It shouldn't have made her sad, but it did. All the dreams, all the hopes, all those long-ago college imaginings were gone, but there was still a part of her that wanted something different than what she had. A husband. Children. The Victorian farmhouse and white picket fence. Cookies in the oven. Thanksgiving meals shared with family.

There was nothing wrong with that, was there?

Of course there wasn't.

After all, it wasn't as if she weren't thankful for the life she'd created in Savannah. She was. She had friends, a career she loved, plenty of things to occupy her time. Lately it just didn't seem like quite enough.

Lately?

Up until last night she'd been happy and satisfied with her life.

Up until she'd seen Seth again.

She grimaced and tapped her fingers against the steering wheel, frustrated with her thoughts and her melancholy mood. It wasn't like her to dwell on what she didn't have. Once she finished this job, things would get back to normal, and she'd feel more herself.

She hoped.

But as she pulled into Dee's driveway, she had the unsettling feeling that her life was changing and that no matter how much she might want to think differently, Seth was going to be a part of it.

Seth and the child he'd had with the woman he'd married after he'd broken Lauren's heart.

"Whatever You've got planned, Lord, I hope it's not a repeat of the past. I've got no desire to have my heart stomped to bits again."

Ever.

And she wouldn't.

She tried to convince herself of that as she went into the carriage house and e-mailed the menus to Seth.

SEVEN

Monday mornings were never easy and this one was worse than usual. Seth ran a hand over his hair and bit back impatience as his son dawdled over a bowl of gluten-free cereal and soy milk.

"Jake, we've got to get moving."

"I don't feel good, Dad. I think I need to stay home."

"Your temperature is normal, you're not congested—"

"It's my stomach." As if to prove his point, Jake shoved the cereal away.

"We both know your stomach is fine." Seth straightened his tie, grabbed his briefcase. He was meeting with a client at nine. He had to get his son out the door before then.

"But—"

"Look, Jake, it's only the third week of school. You can't start skipping days this early in the year."

"But it's pizza day. All the kids are going to be eating it, and I'm going to have to eat a bagged lunch."

"I'm sure you won't be the only kid who isn't eating pizza today."

"I'm the only one out of all my friends who won't be eating it. Matt and Ryan both said they were going to buy lunch today. Jesse always buys lunch." Jake's glum expression made Seth wish he could let his son stay home. Unfortunately, this battle couldn't be conceded. If he let Jake stay home today, they'd have the same argument tomorrow.

"Your friends know about your food allergies. They're not going to make an issue of it."

"They always make an issue of it. Telling me they feel sorry for me and saying how great the pizza is. I don't feel like listening to it today."

"Well, you're going to have to. Today is a school day, and you're going to be at school. Now go get your stuff, so we can get out of here."

"All right." Jake shuffled out of the kitchen and grabbed his backpack, his slumped shoulders saying more than words just how much he didn't want to go to school. Another Monday. Another battle about food.

"Is it really that bad, Jake?"

"No, but it sure feels like it is."

"If you stop worrying about being different, you'll realize that you really aren't."

"I *am* different, Dad."

"So is every other kid in school."

"I know. We're all different. God made us all in a unique way and for a unique purpose. You've told me that a hundred times, but I still don't want to go to school today."

"And I'm still going to have to make you go." Seth ruffled his son's hair and urged him toward the front door. "Get your shoes on and let's get out of here."

Jake obeyed, dragging his feet as he went. "Do you

think Miss Lauren will be able to make the brownies soon? Maybe I can take some of them to school with me. Then while everyone else is eating pizza I can have brownies."

"She was supposed to send the menus yesterday. I'll check my e-mail later and see if she remembered to include brownies."

"Can you do it now?"

"If you don't miss the bus, I can check it as soon as you're gone."

"Thanks, Dad. You're the best." Jake threw thin arms around Seth's waist and squeezed hard.

This was what fatherhood was all about. These moments when your child threw his arms around you and made you feel like a hero.

Seth smiled, hugging Jake back, enjoying the moment. "Remember that next time I make you clean your room instead of playing video games."

"I will." Jake trudged out the door, heading across the yard to the school bus that was just pulling up. A final wave and the bus door closed.

Seth waited until it pulled away, then went back in the house and booted up his computer, hoping Lauren's e-mail would be there. It was and he opened it up, scanning her brief note and the menus attached. No brownies.

He'd have to call Lauren after his meeting and see if she could come up with something Jake and his friends might enjoy. He wasn't happy about it. Doing so would feel like asking for a favor from someone he'd treated badly, but Seth shoved feelings of guilt aside. Lauren had said she had a brownie recipe. All he'd be doing was reminding her that she'd offered to make it.

So why did it bother him so much?

He was honest enough to admit the reason.

He'd made promises to Lauren, a lot of them. He'd listened to her talk about the kind of life she'd wanted, and he'd agreed he wanted the same. He hadn't. He'd wanted adventure. She'd wanted family. In the end, he hadn't been able to see how those two things could go together. Instead of blaming himself, he'd blamed her, throwing her dreams in her face and watching as they died.

He'd grown up a lot since then.

Getting his law degree, getting married, losing his wife, those things had taught him a lot about life and what was important. Maybe if he'd understood those things a decade ago he wouldn't have broken up with Lauren. Not that it mattered now. He'd done what he'd done. He couldn't regret it. Not when the end result had been Jake.

He pushed thoughts of Lauren and the past aside and got in his car. An estate lawyer, he spent a lot of time visiting elderly clients who were unable to drive to his home office for meetings. Today, he had three meetings set up. The first with Mildred Herndale, an eccentric ninety-year-old, who changed her will almost as often as she changed her hair color. Today, she planned on adding a newly adopted cat to her list of beneficiaries. Seth wasn't quite sure how he felt about that.

By the time he finished with the now purple-haired Mildred, he was desperate for a cup of strong, black coffee. A quick stop at the Half Joe shouldn't put him behind schedule.

He parallel parked in front of the building, hurried inside to the counter. "Just a cup of coffee."

"You sure? We just took a pan of cream cheese muffins out of the oven. They'd go good with a cup of joe." The tall gangly kid behind the counter had four earrings in one ear and a stud in his nose. Other than that, he seemed clean-cut and pleasant, his suggestive selling technique reminding Seth that he hadn't had time to eat breakfast.

"I'll take a muffin, too."

"For here?"

"To go." He grabbed the bag, turned to leave and caught a glimpse of dark hair, pale skin, a very familiar profile.

Lauren. Hunkered down over a laptop and biting into what looked like the same type of muffin Seth had just bought.

Ignore her. Turn around and walk away.

But even as his head gave the orders, his feet were skirting chairs and sofas and students and bringing him ever closer to Lauren.

"Is it as good as the guy at the counter said?"

At his question, she startled, glancing up from the computer and meeting his gaze, her cheeks going from pale to pink. "What?"

"I was wondering if the muffin was as good as the guy at the counter said it would be."

"Better." She smiled and for a moment Seth was a kid, sitting across the lunch table at school, looking at the new girl and wondering how many of the guys on the football team would be asking her out in the next week, determined to be the first.

"Then maybe I should eat mine now." He dropped down into the chair next to hers and caught a whiff of some exotic perfume. Spices and flowers, hot breezes and blue oceans. Unexpected. Surprising. Lauren?

He leaned in close, inhaled. Yep. It was definitely Lauren's perfume. "Nice scent."

"That's what Dee says. I'm not sure it's me."

"Let me guess. She gave it to you as a gift and since you're staying with her you feel obligated to wear it."

"Actually, I bought it for myself when I was in Paris. Dee loved it and I gave it to her, but every time I visit her she insists I wear it."

Paris and Lauren. The two wouldn't quite connect in Seth's mind. "When were you in Paris?"

"I attended a culinary school there right after college. Last year I was invited to return to teach a workshop on allergen-free cooking."

"I'm surprised."

"Why?" She watched him through clear, blue eyes, and he wasn't sure how to answer.

He *shouldn't* be surprised at her success. Lauren had always been smart, driven and passionate about what she believed in. The fact that she moved toward her goals with slow deliberation rather than reckless abandon didn't mean she couldn't achieve whatever she set her mind to. That was another thing he hadn't realized until years after he'd broken up with her. "I don't know. I guess I pictured you married, raising kids, having that Victorian farmhouse you always talked about. The white picket fence. Cookies and pies in the oven."

"Homemade bread on the counters." She smiled, the expression more wistful than happy. "Those were my old goals. I made new ones." *After you broke your promises and my heart.*

She didn't add the rest, but he could hear the words as clearly as if she had. "Lola—"

"Have you seen the Web site that just launched?" She cut him off, her words firm, her eyes shouting a warning to back off as she gestured toward her laptop screen.

He wanted to ignore it, but the anger in her eyes told him backing off would be the best choice. "No. What is it?" He leaned forward, scanning the Web page—Magnolia Falls: Where Are They Now.

"Just a way of contacting old friends. People can sign the guest book and leave contact information if they'd like. We're hoping to hear from some missing alumni." Her words spilled out as if she hoped that filling the moment with words would keep Seth from returning to subjects she'd rather not discuss.

"Missing?"

"Maybe not missing so much as drifted away. Magnolia College is a small school with a strong alumni association. It would be nice to find some of the people we've lost contact with."

People like Ellen, people who'd moved on with their lives and cut ties with the school, with friends and with family. He couldn't imagine his half sister bothering to look at the Web site, let alone sign a guest book. Then again, two weeks ago he wouldn't have imagined that he'd be sitting in the Half Joe with Lauren. "The guest book is for public viewing?"

"Yes. The idea is simply to help old friends reconnect."

"It's a good one."

"I can't take credit for it. Some of my friends and I thought it up after our ten-year reunion."

"Friends. I'm guessing that would be Steff, Jennifer, Cassie, Kate and Dee. You six always were quite a team."

"We still are." Lauren closed the computer and stood, wiping crumbs from faded denim jeans. "I'd better head out. Did you and your son have a chance to look at the menus I put together?"

"I did. They look great, but Jake was hoping you could make brownies."

"I will, but those are my gift to him and aren't part of the services you've paid for."

"You don't have to do that, Lauren. I'm happy to pay extra."

"Like I said, there's no charge. I've got to go. Call me once you've decided on a time and a day to make the meals."

"How long will it take?"

"A few hours."

"How about Wednesday around six?"

"That's fine. I'll see you then." She was moving toward the door, and Seth followed, strangely reluctant to let her go. She was Lauren, but different. Intriguing. Beguiling. Worrisome.

Sunlight gleamed off her deep brown hair, painting gold and chestnut highlights in the curls that cascaded from her ponytail. He'd run his fingers through that hair years ago, had looked into vibrant blue eyes and made promises that he'd been sure he'd never break.

Of course he *had* broken them, and life had played out in moments of excitement, joy and sorrow that didn't include the girl he'd thought he'd love forever.

"I've missed you, Lauren. It's good to finally see you again."

She turned to face him, her hand on the door of a bright yellow, vintage Mustang. "What do you want, Seth? Besides menus and meals, I mean. Because whatever it is, I can't give it to you."

"I don't want anything except a chance to get to know the person you've become."

"Why?" She leaned against the car, her face devoid of emotion.

"Because we used to be friends. I'd like to know what's been going on in your life."

"Seth, we were more than friends. Now we're not. You're my client. That being the case, I don't think you need to know anything at all about my life." She opened the door and slid into her car, pulling out onto Main Street before Seth even had time to register what she'd said.

When he did, he couldn't help smiling. The Lauren he'd known never would have been so blunt. He was glad to see she'd learned how to stand up for herself, glad to know that she'd grown more sure of who she was and what she wanted.

Problem was, the more he saw of who she'd become, the more he wanted to know about her. That didn't seem like a good thing. It also didn't seem like something he could stop. He might want to deny it, but he was intrigued by Lauren and getting to know her was something he definitely planned to do. What that meant he couldn't quite decide, and right now wasn't the time to think about it. He had other clients to meet. More paperwork to file. A few phone calls to make.

He needed to put Lauren out of his mind and focus on today. There'd be time enough to decide what was happening between them Wednesday.

The thought made him smile again. Lauren wouldn't want to know that he'd put the two of them together in a sentence let alone that he was wondering what might still be between them. There was something, though. Maybe just memories and nostalgia. Maybe something more. Either way, Seth wasn't going to turn his back on it. He had a feeling that wasn't something that Lauren was going to like.

He climbed inside his car and started toward his next appointment, glancing at the dashboard clock and shaking his head. He'd spent a lot more time in the Half Joe than he'd intended. If he didn't hurry he'd be late to his next appointment. Lately, it seemed he was running full tilt and getting nowhere fast. Eventually things would slow down, but he didn't think it would be any time soon. Since the remains had been found beneath the library sidewalk, Seth had almost doubled his client list. Maybe news of the woman's death had made other people consider their own mortality.

It certainly had Seth thinking about time passing. Ten years gone in the blink of an eye. Ten years since he'd seen his half sister, Ellen. According to his parents, she'd washed her hands of the family a few weeks after Seth's wife passed away. For his part, Seth had been too caught up in grief and in caring for his son to think much about her absence. Ellen had always been a wanderer. This time, though, her wandering hadn't brought her back home.

Seth had tried to contact her several times over the past few years, but hadn't been able to find her. Even that hadn't alarmed him. The body beneath the sidewalk did, though. A body that had been hidden for ten years. Exactly the amount of time Ellen had been missing.

The thought filled him with cold dread. If the police

could extract DNA from the remains, Seth would be tested to see if there was a match. Until then, he'd keep hoping Ellen was alive and well and keep praying she'd get in touch with him soon.

EIGHT

Wednesday came too soon for Lauren's peace of mind. By five o'clock she'd nearly talked herself into canceling her appointment with Seth. Only his son's dietary needs and her own inability to back out on an obligation kept her moving as she packed bags of ingredients, grabbed her purse and laptop and stepped out the carriage house door. The evening was balmy, the sky clear blue, the scent of honeysuckle heavy in the air.

"You're heading out, I see." Dee called out from an open upstairs window, and Lauren glanced up at her sister.

"Unless you can think of a good excuse for me to stay here."

"Are you kidding? This is the most excitement you've had in your life in years. Seth is a jerk, but he's a hunky jerk. And who knows? Maybe he's changed. So, far be it from me to do anything to keep you from your appointment."

"I've had plenty of excitement in the past few years. Not that what I'm doing tonight qualifies as excitement. It's a job, and I'm doing it during my vacation. That's about as thrilling as homework on the weekend used to be."

"You've got a point, but I still think it's exciting. Maybe even a little romantic."

"Romantic? You seem to be forgetting who I'm cooking these meals for."

"Not for a minute. That's why it's romantic. Two young lovers separated by poor choices and time, reconnect at a fund-raiser dinner and realize—"

"Don't you dare say it, Dee. My life is not a movie of the week, and there is nothing romantic about cooking a few meals for Seth and his son." Lauren hadn't meant the words to be so vehement, but they were, and she decided she didn't need to make excuses for it.

"Hey, chill, sis. I was kidding. I'd have to ship you back to Savannah if I really thought you had any interest in renewing your relationship with Seth."

"Sorry. I didn't mean to snap. It's just been a stress-ful few days."

"Yeah, your vacation hasn't exactly turned out the way you planned."

"No, but I figure there's a reason for everything. There must be a reason for this, too." She wasn't sure what it might be, but she had to trust that God's purpose would eventually become clear.

"When you find out what it is, let me know." There was a tinge of cynicism in Dee's tone, but Lauren chose to ignore it. Her sister's feelings about church and religion were something that she hadn't been able to change. Trying had put a wedge between them, and eventually Lauren had realized it was better to let God do whatever work He would in her sister's life than risk severing their relation-ship completely.

"You know I will."

"Feel free to come in and tell me how things went when you're finished."

"I'll probably be late."

"And I'll probably be up. See you then." Dee disappeared, and Lauren hurried around the front of the house. The sun was still high above the trees as she pulled out of the driveway, the warm air that blew in the open window carrying the thick scent of freshly mown grass with it. A beautiful evening and she was about to spend it with a man who'd taken her heart and stomped it to pieces. That wasn't a good thing by any stretch of the imagination. She should be heading out for the exciting evening Dee had joked about. Romance. Companionship. The thrill of attraction.

Ha! As if she'd had time for any of that in the past few years. Well maybe she'd *make* the time. Maybe she'd go back to Savannah and take Marcus Darby up on his dinner invitation. An intelligent, handsome doctor who attended her church, Marcus was everything any woman would want and Lauren had been told more than once that she shouldn't let him slip through her fingers.

So she wouldn't.

Lauren let out an unladylike snort and tried to picture herself getting back into the dating scene. Been there. Done that. Had no desire to repeat the mistake. The fact that she was even thinking about it proved how much seeing Seth again had affected her. Fortunately, she'd be able to fulfill her obligation tonight and put this entire debacle behind her.

The door to Seth's house flew open as she pulled into the driveway. Before she could get out of the car, Jake was there. She smiled at him as she grabbed a bag from the backseat and got out. "Hi, Jake."

"Hi. Cool car."

"I think so. Want to help get these things inside?"

"Sure."

"Good. Grab my laptop off the seat and follow me. We've got a lot of work to do. Is your dad inside?"

"He got stuck at a meeting, but he'll be home soon."

"That's okay. We can get started without him." And maybe finish before he returned. Wouldn't that be nice?

"Hi, Lauren." Reese appeared at the doorway as Jake and Lauren moved up the porch steps, her hair pulled back from a face that seemed just a shade too pale. "Come on in. Seth is running late. He said he'd be glad to reschedule if you'd rather come back another time."

"I'll wait. Jake and I can get started on some of the prep work and sample some of the brownies I brought."

"Great!" Jake ran toward the kitchen, and Lauren started after him, stopping when Reese put a hand on her arm.

"Jake hasn't eaten dinner yet. I'd rather he not have sweets right now." Something hot and bright was in her eyes. Anger? Irritation? Jealousy?

Lauren didn't know, and it really didn't matter. Reese's problems had nothing to do with her, and Lauren had no need to force this particular issue. "That's fine."

"And I'm not sure if Seth really wants you to get started without him. I really think it might be better if you come back another night."

A few years ago, Lauren might have done exactly what Reese seemed to want her to do, but this wasn't a few years ago and she wasn't walking away and having to return another night. Especially since she was anxious to get this done and over with. "Seth and I both have busy schedules, and I'm sure he'll understand that I can't re-schedule easily."

"Suit yourself." Her smile was as fake as the pink Christmas tree Lauren had seen in a Savannah department store last December.

But Lauren hadn't built her reputation as a personal chef by letting the attitudes of others bother her. "Why don't you come in and work with Jake and me? I'm sure you know where all the cooking utensils are."

At her words, Reese softened a little, her tense smile easing. "I'd be glad to help you find what you need, but then I've got to get back to work. I've got a major English paper due tomorrow, and it's not finished yet."

"Are you graduating soon?"

"Next year. If things go well I'll get a job teaching here in Magnolia Falls."

"Elementary school?"

"No. Middle. I like younger kids, but math is my thing and Magnolia Middle is always looking for teachers."

"Have you lived here all your life?"

"Actually, I moved here to attend Magnolia College but I love it. I've got friends. Seth and Jake have become family. It's a good place to be."

Family? Interesting choice of words.

Obviously, Reese was making a point about her position in the Chartrand household. Somehow, though, Lauren couldn't imagine Seth being romantically involved with a woman who was still in college. At least not one that was as young as Reese seemed to be.

Of course, if someone had asked her ten years ago, she would have insisted that there was no way she and Seth would break up. Here she was a decade later, standing two feet from a photo of the woman he'd married.

"Can I have one of the brownies now?" Jake called out from the kitchen, and Lauren moved toward him determined to put Reese's not so subtle hints out of her mind. She was here to cook and that's what she planned to do.

Seth pushed open the front door and stepped into the fragrant aroma of home cooking. Onions. Garlic. Maybe tomato. Whatever it was smelled delicious.

"Dad!" Jake raced from the kitchen, his cheeks glowing, his eyes bright. "You're not going to believe what Lauren made!"

"Miss Lauren."

"You're not going to believe it, Dad."

"Brownies?"

"And something even better. Pizza!"

"Yeah?" He glanced up to see Lauren hovering in the doorway. "I think you've made my son's week."

"We've had fun together." She brushed off his compliment. "I hope you don't mind, but I went ahead and started without you."

"I'm glad you did. I don't want to take up more of your time than necessary."

"It's time you've paid for, so don't worry about it."

Ouch! The new Lauren could sure put a person in his place. "Time is always valuable. No matter who is paying for it."

"You're finally home." Reese stepped out of the study, her

blond ponytail slightly crooked, her face a little paler than usual. It looked as though she'd had as rough a day as Seth.

"Yeah, sorry for the delay."

"You don't need to apologize. You know I love being here with Jake." She put a hand on Seth's arm, stared up into his eyes.

"I know, but I'm sure you had plans for this evening." He eased away from her hold, his gaze following Lauren as she moved back into the kitchen.

"None that mattered."

"I'm not sure I believe that." Seth forced his attention back to Reese. "But I'm going to make this up to you. Since I worked late tonight, I'm going to work from home tomorrow. Which means you'll have an entire afternoon and evening to yourself for a change."

"You don't have to do that, Seth."

"Actually, I do. Sometimes I'm more productive here than I am in my office."

"Oh. All right. I guess I'll see you and Jake on Friday then."

"See you then." He held the door open, waited until she got in her car and then started toward the kitchen.

Jake and Lauren were both standing at the sink, their backs to Seth, their heads bent close as Jake ran water over a colander of spinach. Red hair next to brunette. Slim arm next to bony elbow. As he watched, Lauren smiled down at Jake, ruffling his hair and saying something that made Jake laugh. They looked as if they'd been preparing dinners together for years.

The warmth of the kitchen, the rich aroma of the food, the easy companionship between Jake and Lauren stalled the breath in Seth's lungs and made him long for something

that he'd thought he would never want again. A mother for
Jake. A wife to come home to. A female influence in their
all-male world.

"Dad, come look. We're making wedding soup. Miss
Lauren says it's the best."

"I'm sure it is. It's always been one of my favorites." He
met Lauren's eyes, biting back a smile as her cheeks heated.

She turned quickly, grabbing the spinach from the sink,
putting handfuls of it in a large pot on the stove. Tendrils
of hair fell from the bun she'd twisted her hair into, sliding
down the creamy skin at the back of her neck and transporting Seth to another time, another kitchen.

*It was twenty degrees hotter in the Owenses' house than
it had been outside. Or maybe the sweat beading Seth's
forehead was from nerves. He wiped it away, hoping Mrs.
Owens hadn't noticed.*

*"Right through here, Seth. I'm so glad you could come
tonight. My husband and I have been looking forward to
meeting you."*

*"I've been looking forward to meeting you, too." Had
he sounded too eager to please? Not eager enough? What
was a guy supposed to say to the parents of the girl he
wanted to date, anyway? It wasn't as if he'd had much
practice at this. None of the other girls he'd dated had
asked him to meet their folks.*

*Mrs. Owens pushed open a door and gestured into the
room beyond. A kitchen. Lacy curtains. A round table with
a frilly tablecloth and a vase of flowers on it. Lauren
standing in front of a stove, her back to them, a tendril of
hair sliding down the slim line of her neck.*

She turned as they moved into the room, her cheeks pink,

her lips a shade darker, her eyes welcoming him as no one else ever had. And he knew he'd put up with a thousand parent meetings if it meant spending more time with her.

"Taste this, Dad."

Seth took the brownie his son held out to him, pushing aside the past and all its memories.

He'd exchanged his relationship with Lauren for excitement, newness, freedom. In the end, he'd wound up exactly where he'd been afraid she was leading him—settled down, with a house, a child, a small-town life and a career that was more stable than exciting.

The irony was, he'd come to realize that the life Lauren had seemed to offer, the life he'd run from was exactly the life he wanted. But he wouldn't allow himself to question the choices he'd made, the life he'd lived. His choices might not have been the best, but the result of them had been Jake. Because of that, he wouldn't change what he'd done even if he were given the opportunity to go back and live certain moments again.

That was exactly why he was better off keeping his mind in the here and now, and his thoughts off Lauren and all the things that might have been, but weren't.

NINE

Done. Finally. Lauren washed the last pot by hand, dried it and placed it back in the drawer under the stove. The last few hours had passed quickly, Jake's excited chatter driving the evening forward, adding zest and flavor to what might otherwise have been a bland night of cooking.

As if anything could be bland with Seth around.

She yanked off her apron, shoved it into her purse, closed her laptop with a little more force than necessary. Cooking with him in the kitchen had been nerve-racking, his gaze following her as she moved around the room, his attention never wavering as she explained ingredients, pulled up menus on her computer, offered tips on preparing meals ahead of time. She'd been relieved when he'd allowed Jake to stay up late. The little boy's excitement had been the perfect buffer for his father's intensity.

Seth had escorted his son upstairs to bed fifteen minutes ago. Lauren figured she'd set a record for cleaning a kitchen. She glanced around, made sure everything was in place. Then hurried out of the room and down the hall. It was time to go back to Dee's guesthouse and start her vacation.

"Sneaking out without saying goodbye?" Seth moved

down the stairs, his voice as rich as dark chocolate, his eyes deep green and sparkling with amusement.

"I said goodbye."

"To Jake."

True. "I didn't know how long you'd be upstairs, and it's getting late."

"Not so late that you had to rush away."

"I'm not rushing. I'm finished. The meals are cooked. You've got extra menu ideas. Ingredients. Everything you need to prepare a lot of Jake's favorite foods." She pulled open the door and stepped out into balmy night air. "Is there something else you need?"

"I think I already told you what that was."

"And I think I already told you how I feel about it."

"Maybe I'm hoping you changed your mind." He leaned against the porch railing, six foot one of handsome, his eyes gleaming in the dim overhead light.

What did he think her reaction to his words would be? What did he hope she'd say?

Obviously not what Lauren planned to say—she'd moved on with her life and put their relationship behind her. She had no intention of revisiting it again.

That *was* what she was going to say, wasn't it?

Of course it was.

There was no way she could even consider anything else.

"I'm not the kind of person who changes her mind."

His gaze didn't leave her face as he reached out and grabbed her hand, tugging her toward him before she could retreat down the stairs. "You don't have to change your mind, Lola. You just have to let things happen."

Her skin warmed beneath his palm, her pulse leaping

the way it had when she'd been sixteen and walking through the hallways at school, Seth's hand wrapped around hers. "I am letting things happen, Seth. I'm letting myself go home after a very long day, and I'm going to let myself start a well-deserved vacation." She tugged her hand from his, started down the steps, trying to calm the wild beating of her heart.

"You're letting yourself run away from what you're feeling."

She whirled to face him again. "I'm not feeling anything but irritation that you'd suggest we get to know each other again. I learned everything I needed to know about you when you broke up with me." To her disgust, her voice shook on the last word.

"Lauren, I never meant to hurt you."

"But you did, Seth. I won't forget that." She climbed in the Mustang before he could say more, telling herself she was angry. Not sad, not wistful, not regretting the past. Angry.

No. Not even that. Being angry would mean feeling something for Seth, and she was determined not to feel anything. Her hands tightened on the steering wheel, the blackness of the night beyond the car's headlights reflecting her dark mood. This was what she got for agreeing to do something she didn't want to do. If she'd just said no to Steff, she'd still be in Savannah with Seth somewhere in the far recesses of her mind.

Up ahead, Dee's house beckoned, a light shining in an upstairs window. Dee was awake, just like she'd said she would be, but Lauren had no intention of going in the house. She wasn't in the mood for conversation, wasn't in the mood for trying to explain the way she felt when she was with Seth. She wasn't even sure she *could* explain it. Sorrow, anger, interest. It was a mixed bag of emotions that Lauren would rather shove under a sofa somewhere than explore.

She sighed, pulling around the back of the house and parking in front of the small carriage house at the edge of the property. She'd left the light above the front door on, but now it was out, the large bushes on either side casting deep gray shadows over what should have been a well-lit area. Strange. Or maybe not. The carriage house wasn't used often. The lightbulb had probably burned out.

As Lauren watched, the shadows shifted and changed, the slight breeze tickling leaves so that they rustled and swayed. A warning shivered along her spine and lodged at the base of her skull, but she pushed it aside. Bad things didn't happen in small-town Georgia.

Then what do you call a woman buried beneath a sidewalk for ten years? What do you call a murderer wandering free?

The questions whispered through her mind as she grabbed her laptop and purse and stepped out of the Mustang. She ignored them. After all, there was no evidence that the deceased had been murdered and no reason to think that a murderer had been living in Magnolia Falls for the past ten years.

Right?

Right.

The breeze rustled the leaves again and touched Lauren's hair and skin with ghostly fingers that made her shiver. She could almost imagine someone watching from the darkened windows of the carriage house or peering from the shadowy corners. Almost hear the raspy breath of the watcher as he waited to pounce.

"Stop it!" She hissed the words, refusing to allow her imagination to take hold, refusing to revert to the timid mousy creature she'd once been. Ten years living alone, ten years building her reputation as a premier Savannah chef, ten years learning who she was and where she belonged had made her strong. Independent. A woman who didn't panic, didn't overreact, and did *not* allow her imagination to get the better of her.

She shoved open the carriage house door, flicked on the living room light and froze. Shredded fabric. White stuffing pulled from once-pristine sofa and chairs. Books strewn across paint-splattered hardwood floor. Framed photos trampled and torn. To the left, the bathroom door yawned open, light spilling across the floor and reflecting off a slick, wet substance that might have been shampoo, lotion, *blood*. To the right, the lone bedroom door was closed. She knew she'd left it open.

A sound drifted into the silence. Feet shuffling across the bedroom floor? The brush of someone's arm against the wall? Fabric rustling as a killer moved in?

Lauren didn't wait to hear more. She stumbled backward, away from the subtle sound and from the chaos, danger a hot breath against her neck.

Someone was there, coming out of the bedroom, following her across the yard. Lauren bypassed the back door, sprinting toward the front of the house and screaming Dee's name. Grass crunched beneath her feet, the fragrant scent of it surrounding her, terror chasing her. The front door of Dee's house flew open as Lauren sprinted up the front stairs.

"What is it? What's going on?" Dee's face was drained of color, her eyes stark blue in a bloodless face.

Lauren grabbed her arm, yanking her into the house and slamming the door. "Someone was in the carriage house."

"What? What are you talking about, Lauren?"

"The carriage house. It's been torn apart. I heard someone in the bedroom. We've got to call the police."

"Lock the door. I'll get the phone." Dee hurried down the hall and Lauren pulled the bolt on the door, her hands— her entire body—shaking.

The bad things she hadn't wanted to believe could happen in small-town Georgia had happened, and her perspective had altered, the safe cocoon she'd imagined herself in suddenly not so safe, the familiar comforting world, not familiar at all.

"The police are on their way. We're to stay in here until they arrive." Dee reappeared, her face even more pale than it had been before. "Are you okay?"

"Yes." Her voice shook, and Dee grabbed her arm, pulling her toward the stairs.

"Let's go to my room. Just in case."

"In case what?"

"In case whoever was in the carriage house decides to try and get inside here. I'd rather have another locked door between us."

Lauren couldn't agree more. She hurried up the stairs after her sister, following her into the master bedroom and collapsing onto the bed. "I can't believe this is happening."

"Me, neither."

"Whoever was in the carriage house was there awhile. The entire place is wrecked. Sofa. Chairs. Bathroom."

"Was the door unlocked?"

"Not when I left and not when I got home."

"Maybe the back door?"

"Dee, you know how careful I am about locking up."

"So maybe whoever it was broke a window."

"Did you hear anything while I was gone?"

"Nothing."

"He got in somehow. I guess we'll find out how, once the police get here." Lauren shivered, hugging her arms tight around her waist. "I'm really sorry about this, Dee."

"Sorry about what? You didn't break into the carriage house, and you didn't trash it." Dee stood, paced to the window. "I hear sirens."

"Do you see police cars?"

"Not yet. I think…"

"What?"

"Come here. Quick!" Dee hissed the command, gesturing Lauren to the window.

She peered out, the night eerie and still beyond the glass. Streetlights cast yellowish light onto pavement and grass, but Lauren could see nothing out of the ordinary. "What is it? What did you see?"

"Over there. Across the street near that big tree. I think there's someone standing in the shadows."

Lauren leaned closer to the glass, staring at the large magnolia tree, trying to distinguish shadow from solid form. Was that a person standing beneath the branches of the tree? She couldn't tell, wasn't sure. The sirens crescendoed to a screaming frenzy, and, as Lauren watched, the shadow separated from the cover of the trees. Black against black, menacing. Real. Staring up toward Lauren and Dee before slipping away into the darkness beyond the streetlight's glow.

"Someone was out there."

"Yeah." Dee's voice sounded shaky, and Lauren put an arm around her shoulder needing the contact as much as she thought her sister did.

"But he's gone now."

"Not before he made sure we knew he was there. That's creepy."

"And scary."

"And just plain weird."

Blue-and-white lights flashed as a police car sped into view.

"Finally!" Dee rushed for the door and Lauren followed, a sense of dread knotting her stomach and filling her with the kind of fear that went beyond anything she'd ever experienced before. Someone had been in the carriage house, had been standing across the street from Dee's house, watching. Why? Lauren could only pray the police would figure it out quickly. She didn't think she'd feel safe again until they did.

TEN

It didn't take long for the police to check the guesthouse and dust for prints. What they discovered wasn't nearly enough for Lauren's peace of mind. A jimmied back door. A huge mess. No fingerprints. No evidence. Life would have been a lot easier if they'd found the vandal waiting to turn himself in.

She took a sip of steaming coffee and set the cup down on Dee's dining room table. Her eyes were gritty, her head ached and she wanted to crawl into bed and forget the day had ever happened. Unfortunately, she didn't think that would be happening any time soon.

"You're sure you didn't see any details of the person's face when you looked out the window?" Detective Anderson glanced up from his notepad, his dark gaze sympathetic, but sharp as if he were searching for some truth that Lauren or Dee might be hiding. Stiff-uniformed, tall and rangy, the detective seemed determined to leave no stone unturned.

Which was fine with Lauren. The sooner they caught the vandal and put him in jail, the happier she'd be. "No. It was too dark."

"No gut feeling about whether it was a male or female?"

"Nothing."

"And there's no one you can think of who might have something against you? No work rivalry? No jealous ex-boyfriend?"

"Detective, I only *wish* my life were that exciting." Dee tapped her fingers against the table, her blond hair falling forward over her shoulder, her eyes shadowed. As much as she was trying to act upbeat and unconcerned, Lauren could sense her tension and worry.

"Actually, ma'am, it is." He jotted a note, glanced at Lauren.

"How about you?"

"No one I can think of."

"You said you're a personal chef. Do you have any clients that are unhappy with you? Maybe someone who has an ax to grind?"

"Not that I know of. Even if one of them did, they wouldn't have known to find me here. I told my clients I'd be out of town, but not where I was going."

He nodded, stood. "Here's what I'm thinking right now. Some kid decided to break into the guesthouse hoping to find some money or valuables."

"The only thing of value I brought was my laptop, and I didn't leave it in the carriage house when I went out tonight."

"Exactly. Kid breaks in, doesn't find anything, and gets mad. Busts up the couch and chairs. Messes the place up and leaves."

"Why?"

"Because that's what kids who are looking for trouble do. Sad to say, it's something I see all the time."

"But he was still there when I got home. I heard him in the bedroom."

"He probably heard you drive up and was scared out of his mind, thinking he was going to get caught."

"Then why not get out and run? Why stick around staring at Dee's house?" Lauren knew the detective couldn't answer her question, but it was one she'd been asking herself for the past hour.

"We don't know that he did, ma'am. Anyone could have been standing across the street."

True, but Lauren had a feeling that the person she'd seen was the same one who'd torn apart the carriage house. She also had a feeling what had happened tonight was a lot more personal than what the officer had just described. "I understand what you're saying, Detective Anderson, but I really do think the person who was in the carriage house was standing outside staring up at Dee and me."

"And you may be right. I'm not ruling anything out. I want to assure you both that there will be a thorough investigation. We plan to find the person responsible, whether that person is a kid or someone else entirely."

"We appreciate it, detective. Is there anything we can do to help?" Dee looked wan and tired, and Lauren wondered if there was more than vandalism on her sister's mind.

"If you think of anyone who might be holding a grudge against either of you, you can give me a call. Here's my card." He handed it to Dee, then moved toward the front door. "It might be best if you get new locks on the carriage house doors. The ones you have aren't going to keep anyone out. You might also want to get a security system installed.

I see you've got one here. You can probably get the same company to come out and hook your carriage house up."

"I'll have them come out tomorrow."

"Call the station if there's any more trouble."

"We will."

"I'll be in touch." Detective Anderson moved down the driveway and got into his cruiser.

Lauren waited until he drove away, then closed the door, turning to face her sister. "I guess we'd better start cleaning up the carriage house." Even though the thought of it made her shudder.

"Wrong." Dee grabbed her arm and pulled her back into the dining room. "We're not going to clean the carriage house. We're not going to *think* about the carriage house."

"I suppose you've got something else planned."

"Don't I always?"

"Yes. So? What is it?"

"First, we're going to make some more coffee. Then we're going to pull out my emergency supply of chocolate and spend some time looking at the guest book entries for the Web site while we pig out. After that, you're going to sleep in my guest room. We'll deal with everything else tomorrow."

"Bed sounds good. The rest of it I'm not up for."

"Do you really think you're going to be able to sleep right now?"

"Probably not."

"Me, neither. So, we'll do something to take our minds off of what happened tonight."

"Sounds like a plan."

"Good. You boot up my computer, and I'll get the chocolate."

Lauren smiled as she did what her sister suggested. Only twelve months apart, she and Dee had always been close. Still, they were more different than they were alike. Dee as open and gregarious as Lauren tended to be quiet and reserved. Popular and pretty, Dee had always been the center of every social activity in school and in college. Lauren, on the other hand, had been content to have a few close friends.

And Seth.

But she wasn't going to think about Seth. Or the trashed carriage house. Or the person stepping from the shadows of the magnolia tree and staring up at her.

She shuddered, pulling up her e-mails and scrolling through them to distract herself.

"Anything from the Web site yet?" Dee threw a handful of mini candy bars on the table in front of her.

"Actually, yes. Angela Heaton posted a guest book entry."

"Really? That's great. One less missing alumni. What's she say?"

"She's Angela Gray, now. Got married a few years back. Has two kids. They live in Arizona."

"Is she teaching?"

"She doesn't say."

"Did she leave an address?"

"E-mail."

"I'll have to contact her and see how life has been." Dee grabbed a chocolate and unwrapped it. "Anyone else?"

"At least twenty others, but it looks like they're from people who either came to the reunion, or graduated in a different year."

"Well, one response from our graduating class is better

than none. At least we know Angela isn't…" Her voice trailed off and she shook her head, but Lauren knew exactly what she'd been thinking. At least Angela wasn't dead.

"I'm sure we'll hear from everyone else soon." At least she hoped they would. Knowing that some poor woman had been buried beneath a sidewalk for ten years was bad enough. Finding out it was someone she'd talked to, shared her college years with would be even worse.

"We'll see. People get busy after college. Life takes off and the next thing you know it's ten years later and you've forgotten more than you remember about college and the people who were there. Have a chocolate." She tossed one across the table, and Lauren caught it.

"We've managed to stay close to most of our college buddies."

"True. I guess we're fortunate. Of course, there are some people we might just as soon keep far away from." Dee popped another chocolate in her mouth. "Speaking of which, how did things go tonight?"

"Aside from the trashed carriage house, fine."

"That doesn't tell me much."

"That's because there's not much to tell. I went to Seth's place. I cooked a bunch of meals. I left."

"You're a brat, you know that?"

"And you're nosy."

Dee laughed. "Guilty, but you've got to admit, it's intriguing."

"No, I don't. There's nothing intriguing about seeing Seth again. I'm just glad it's over and I can move on."

"Are you?" The laughter had faded from Dee's eyes, and she leaned toward Lauren.

"Of course."

"Too bad."

"Too bad? You've never liked Seth. You've called him a jerk at least twice since Friday night."

"You're right about me calling him a jerk. You're wrong about me not liking him. I always liked Seth. He just overshadowed you when you were younger."

"So did you."

"Yeah, well I was your older sister. That's what I was supposed to do. And now I couldn't overshadow you if I tried. We're both successful, self-assured, confident. Neither of us will let ourselves be doormats under the heel of some guy's ego."

"Seth never treated me a like a doormat."

"Maybe not, but he sure didn't always treat you like you were special."

"We were kids."

"And now you're grown and spending a lot of time defending a man you never plan to see again."

"I'm not defending him, I'm just…" Defending him. Lauren shook her head and grabbed another chocolate. "What was between me and Seth was a long time ago. He's changed. I've changed. I guess I just don't see any reason to rehash the past."

"You're right. Sorry."

"You're apologizing? What happened tonight must have really shaken you." Lauren scrolled down her list of e-mails, clicked open one, scanned it.

"Didn't it shake you up?"

"Yeah, that's why I'm glad you've decided I'm staying in your spare room tonight. No way would I want to sleep in the carriage house." She opened another e-mail, started reading it. "This is odd."

"What?" Dee came around the table and stood behind Lauren, leaning over her shoulder to look at the computer screen.

"This e-mail. Not everyone at Magnolia College is what he seems. What's that supposed to mean?"

"Got me. Who's it from."

"Anonymous."

"Clever pseudonym." Dee's dry humor did nothing to ease the dread that tied Lauren's stomach in knots.

"Do you think this has anything to do with the body the police found?"

"I think it's someone's idea of a joke."

"I don't know, Dee. It seems…sinister."

"Sinister is someone breaking into the carriage house and trashing it. What you've got there is nothing more than silly."

"Maybe they're connected."

"What?" Dee moved back to her chair.

"The vandalism and this e-mail."

"Because they happened on the same day? I don't think so, Laur. It's just a coincidence."

Maybe, but what if it wasn't? What if there was something going on that was a lot more dangerous than kids playing pranks. "I think we'd better let the police decide that."

"Suit yourself, but don't be surprised if they tell you exactly what I just did."

"Detective Anderson did say to contact him if anything else happened."

"You'll have to let me know what he says." Dee stood and stretched. "I don't know about you, but I'm all chocolated out. I think I'm going to head off to bed. I've got an early meeting tomorrow. I can't be late for it."

"I'm ready for bed, too." She wasn't sure she'd be able to sleep, though. Too much to think about. Too many worries.

"You can take the room at the top of the stairs. I'll be out of the house before dawn. Grab what you want from the kitchen. I think I've got some eggs and bread. Would you mind being here when the security company comes by? I don't think I'll be able to come home, and I don't want to put off getting the system installed."

"Sure. Call me and let me know when, and I'll be here."

"Thanks. I'll handle cleanup in the guesthouse when I get home."

Lauren nodded, following her sister up the stairs. Telling Dee that she'd be happy to do the cleanup would be a waste of time. Knowing her sister, she'd insist on staying home to help and that wasn't necessary. Tomorrow, Lauren would take care of it and tell Dee after she was finished.

The spare room was bright and cozy, the sage paint and mahogany furniture giving it a sophisticated air. Dee stood in the doorway, her blue eyes shadowed by fatigue. "I'll get you some pajamas. I don't think either of us wants to go out to get your suitcase."

"I know *I* don't."

By the time Lauren had changed and located a Bible in Dee's study, her eyelids felt weighted, her legs heavy. She wanted to sleep, but each time she closed her eyes images of the trashed carriage house appeared. Reading the Bible, listening to the radio that sat on the bedside table, pacing the room, none of those things helped get her mind off the troubling events of the evening.

How could it be that her mundane life could suddenly have become so filled with trouble? Seth. The carriage house. The strange e-mail. She'd hoped to spend a couple of weeks relaxing and enjoying some time with Dee and her friends. Somehow, she didn't think that was going to happen.

She sighed, flicking off the bedside lamp and staring at the darkened ceiling. This was all part of God's plan. She knew that. Now, if she could just figure out what that plan was, she'd be a lot more relaxed about what the next few days would bring.

"Whatever it is, Lord, I know You're in control, and I trust You to get me through it. Help me to understand Your will for my life so that I can better live it for You."

In a low voice, Lauren finished the prayer, the sense of peace she so often felt in the presence of the Lord filling her. Whatever the future held, God was in it. That, more than locks, security systems or police gave her the sense of safety she needed to sleep.

One by one the lights went out and the house faded into darkness. It would be easy to jimmy the front door, ease into the expansive foyer, creep up the stairs. Easy, but not smart. The sisters were on guard, they might sleep fitfully and wake before the job was done. Better to wait until their guard was down again. Better to enter the house when no one was expecting it. Better to be sure that nothing that was hidden would come to light. The past needed to stay where it was. Dead and buried. This time, that was exactly what was going to happen. Nothing else was acceptable. Nothing else would be allowed.

Across the street, a door opened and a fat little dog

waddled out. It sniffed the air, let out a gruff bark. Then another. Time to go. There'd be another day to finish what had been started.

Permanently.

ELEVEN

True to her word, Dee left the house before dawn. Lauren heard the splash of water and quiet drone of the shower, the soft rustle of Dee's clothes as she went downstairs. Maybe she should go down and have coffee with her sister, but Lauren didn't have the energy to rehash any of last night's events. Today was a new day. The best thing for both herself and her sister was to get the security system, clean up the carriage house and go on with their normal routine. The problem was, things weren't normal. No matter how much Lauren tried to convince herself otherwise, she was sure the anonymous e-mail she'd received and the vandalized carriage house were connected. What she couldn't figure out was how.

She waited until nine, then dialed the number on Detective Anderson's card, sure he'd tell her the e-mail was nothing to worry about.

"Detective Anderson. What can I do for you?"

"Hi, this is Lauren Owens. My sister's carriage house was vandalized last night, and you came by to investigate."

"What can I do for you, Ms. Owens?"

"I received a strange e-mail last night."

"Strange as in threatening?" His voice was sharp, and Lauren's own tension rose.

"Not threatening, just…odd."

"Want to tell me what it said?"

"That not everyone at Magnolia College is what he seems to be."

"That's it?" The sharpness eased from his tone, and he seemed only mildly interested.

"Yes."

"Are you affiliated with the college?"

"No, but some friends and I are running a Web site designed to keep college alumni in touch with one another."

"You've been doing that long?"

"We launched Monday."

"Interesting timing."

"For the Web site?"

"Yeah. What with the body found there a couple of weeks ago."

"That's what sparked the idea. We had our class reunion and some of our graduating class didn't show. We wanted to track everyone down just to make sure they were okay."

"I see."

"You see what?"

"You're playing detective."

"We weren't thinking of it that way."

"Maybe not, but based on the e-mail you got, I'd say you're stirring up trouble."

"Do you think that has something to do with what happened last night?"

"I'm not sure, but I'm not willing to count on it being a coincidence. I'll tell you what. Why don't you stop by the station sometime today? I'll take a statement, and we'll go from there."

"All right. I'll be by this afternoon."

Lauren wasn't sure if she felt better or worse when she hung up the phone. Having the detective take her concerns seriously was great, but it only made her worry more.

Had the Web site stirred up trouble?

She hoped not.

By the time she'd cleaned up the guesthouse and waited for the security system to be installed, it was past noon. Her stomach was growling, her head ached and the phone was ringing off the hook. One call after another from concerned neighbors who'd seen the police arrive the previous night or from friends who'd heard that the police had been there.

Lauren answered half a dozen before giving up and letting Dee's answering machine pick up. After that, she figured she could either sit around feeling guilty for not answering the phone, or she could head to the police station and maybe pick up something to eat on the way there. The second option seemed the better one, and she grabbed her purse and laptop and headed for Magnolia Falls.

The day was bright, the sky crystal blue, the air thick with late-summer warmth. Lauren rolled down the window and hummed along with the radio as she drove into town, doing her best to ignore the dread that had taken up residence in her stomach.

Unfortunately, ignoring it wasn't as easy as she wanted it to be. Wrecked furniture, ripped books, papers strewn everywhere, an intruder slipping out of the carriage house. Image after image flashed through her mind until she felt dizzy with them. Or maybe it was hunger that was making her light-headed. Burt's Pizza was on Main Street, and Lauren pulled into the parking lot, her stomach grumbling as she inhaled the yeasty scent of baking pizza.

She took a seat in a quiet corner of the pizzeria, placing her order and then opening her laptop. There were at least ten more guest book entries that needed approval before being posted. Her heart beat a little faster as she read each, but none seemed unusual. She checked her e-mails, was relieved to find nothing out of the ordinary there, either, and then pulled up the Magnolia Falls: Where Are They Now Web site.

"The Web site looks great." Seth's voice pulled her attention from the computer, and she looked up into deep, green eyes.

Her heart skipped a beat, her breath caught in her throat, her response to him much the same as it had been the first time she'd seen him.

Good thing she was older now. And wiser. "Thank you. I'll tell Jennifer you said so."

"She was the mastermind on this one?"

"She designed it." Lauren turned her attention back to the screen, hoping Seth would get the hint and move on.

"Anyone sitting with you?"

"No." And that's the way she planned to keep it.

"Mind if I do? There aren't any free tables, and I'm not up for eating pizza in my car."

Yes, she did mind, but her mother had raised her to be polite, and Lauren couldn't find it within herself to say what she was thinking. "No. Go ahead."

He slid into the booth across from her, and Lauren told

herself to ignore him. To focus on the Web site and pretend he wasn't there. Of course she didn't listen to her own advice. She snapped the laptop closed, meeting Seth's eyes again and feeling the same jump in her pulse. "Late lunch?"

"Yeah. I had a ten o'clock meeting that took a lot longer than I expected it to. How about you?"

"Just hungry."

"And eating Burt's pizza. I'm surprised."

"Why?"

"You're an expert chef. I'd think you'd be eating something five-star."

"Good food is good food. Burt's pizza is definitely that."

"Better than boxed macaroni any day."

Lauren smiled at that. "I haven't had boxed macaroni since college. That first year, I must have had it twice a week every week." Every time she'd gone to dinner at the apartment Seth had rented off campus.

"Hey, I was young and broke. It was all I could afford."

"Remember the time you tried to fancy it up? I came over for dinner and your whole place smelled like garlic and onion. You mixed in ground beef and put a red rose in a vase on the table." Lauren had been touched, all her worry, all her wondering if Seth might be outgrowing her fading as she stared into his eyes.

"I remember that you choked down every bite. One taste was enough for me."

"I…" Loved him. Hadn't wanted to hurt him. Had thought he'd felt the same about her.

"You what?"

"I didn't think it was that bad."

"It *was* bad. Unlike this pizza. Which is delicious." He

smiled and bit into a slice, his gaze steady and intense. "I heard you had some trouble last night."

"Did you?"

"One of my clients heard about it from a friend who lives in Dee's neighborhood. Is everything okay?"

"Yes. Someone vandalized the guesthouse while I was at your place. Nothing was taken, but the living room furniture was trashed."

"Do the police have any idea who did it?"

"No. They think it was probably kids, but it's hard to say."

"But you have an opinion?"

"No, just a feeling."

"About?"

"Someone made an entry to the guest book on the alumni Web site we're running. It made me wonder if there's something going on. Something more than pranks."

"What'd it say?"

"Nothing awful. Just that not everyone at Magnolia College is who he seems to be."

Seth steepled his fingers under his chin, his expression somber. "On its own, it isn't much. Combined with the vandalism, I think you're right. Something is going on. Have you contacted the police about the e-mail?"

"Yes. I'm heading in to see Detective Anderson when I'm done here."

"Want me to come with you?"

"I don't think I'll need a lawyer today." She smiled, but he didn't return it.

"Even if you did, I'm not a criminal lawyer. My specialty is in estate planning. What I was thinking is that you might want some moral support."

"I'm not fifteen anymore, Seth. I'm fine on my own."

"Yeah, I know you are, but that doesn't mean you wouldn't like some company."

She was tempted. She'd admit that. Having Seth with her would be so much better than going into the police station alone, but she'd fought hard to gain the confidence to go her own way and do her own thing. No way did she plan to backtrack now. "I appreciate the offer, but I'm used to doing things on my own."

"I guess you are. If you need me, though, you know where to find me." They moved toward the door, arms close, steps in sync as if ten years hadn't passed, as if they'd never been apart.

Lauren's throat tightened, her mind spinning back in time. They'd been a good team once upon a time. Too bad it hadn't lasted. "Thanks."

"Listen, before you go, I've got a favor to ask."

"What's that?"

He hesitated, something dark flashing behind his eyes. "Do you remember my sister?"

"Ellen? Sure." What did Seth's half sister, Ellen, have to do with Lauren? Older than her brother by several years, Ellen had seemed to be both volatile and affectionate.

"Then you remember that things weren't always easy between my parents and my sister."

Not easy? They'd been downright difficult. Lauren could remember plenty of heated arguments during her visits with Seth. "I do. Didn't she attend Magnolia College a few years before you?"

"She graduated three years before I started, but did some freelance photography for the college after she graduated."

"That's right. I remember seeing her a few times the year I started attending the school. We may have even shared a pot of macaroni."

She expected Seth to smile at her comment, but he just nodded, his eyes shadowed, his expression grim. "That's right."

"Is she okay?"

"I wish I knew. I haven't seen her in ten years."

Ten years? That wasn't good. It wasn't good at all.

"Ten years is a long time to go without seeing someone."

"You're telling me." He ran a hand over his hair, and Lauren remembered the softness of his thick waves, the spicy scent of his shampoo. "I've tried to track her down through friends, but no one seems to know where she is."

Definitely not good. Could the woman found beneath the sidewalk be Seth's sister? Lauren prayed not. "Your parents must be worried sick."

"Honestly? Ellen was a challenge to them. They didn't understand her, and they didn't approve of her. In some ways, it's probably almost been a relief that she's been gone. I've missed her, though. Worried about her. Hoped that everything was okay and that eventually she'd get in touch with me."

"I'm sorry, Seth. What do you need my help with?"

"Ellen had a lot of friends at college. She may want to reconnect with people she's lost touch with. I've been skimming through the guest book entries on your Web site, but I know you're getting the entries before they're made public. If you get one from Ellen can you let me know? I'm worried that... I'm worried."

He didn't have to say more for Lauren to know what he

was worried about. Ellen gone for ten years. A body hidden for ten years. If she'd made the connection, he had, too. She reached for him, wrapping her arms around his waist, feeling the firm muscles of his abdomen, the tension in him.

She shouldn't be doing this. She shouldn't be hugging him. Shouldn't be comforting him. Shouldn't be agreeing to help. But before they'd dated they'd been friends, connecting in a way that she hadn't forgotten and couldn't ignore. "You think the woman they found is Ellen, don't you?"

"I'm worried it could be."

"It's not." Even as she said it, she knew she couldn't be sure, knew that it was very possible Ellen would never mend the broken relationship with her family.

"I hope you're right, Lola. The thought of Ellen dying alone, maybe scared is eating me up." His arms were around her, warm and strong, his hands resting on her waist, his breath ruffling her hair. Everything about him so different and yet so very familiar. An old friend she hadn't seen in years. A boyfriend she'd pinned all her hopes and dreams on. A man she didn't know, couldn't read, maybe wanted to know.

She eased out of his arms, her heart beating too fast, her breath shallow and uneven. "Ellen was tough and strong, and I have a feeling she's fine. I'll definitely let you know if I hear from her. I'd better go. I've still got things to do."

He nodded, watching her through hooded eyes as she opened the Mustang door and slid inside.

Don't look back at him, Lauren. Don't acknowledge him again. You don't want to look needy, or desperate.

She could almost hear Dee whispering the words in her ear. Somehow, though, her eyes lifted, her gaze settled on

Seth. He smiled, his lips curving in warm invitation, telling her that she could have stayed in his arms forever, that she could have leaned her head against his chest, listened to his heart beat in time with hers as she had so many times when she'd been young.

Eleven years and he still moved her. Still made her long for a Victorian farmhouse, a white picket fence. Children. Cookies baking in the oven. Seth had never wanted those things. He'd wanted a big career. A name. Travel. Adventure.

Funny that each had ended up with what the other wanted.

Or maybe not so funny.

She pulled out of the parking lot, promising herself that she'd put Seth out of her mind, but she knew the truth. Putting Seth out of her mind wasn't possible. The fact was, she was standing at the top of a slippery and very dangerous slope. It wouldn't take much to send her sliding out of control and into trouble.

Maybe she already had.

TWELVE

He shouldn't have asked Lauren to help keep an eye out for e-mails or guest book entries from Ellen. Seth knew that. But sitting across from her at Burt's, looking into her concerned eyes had been so much like old times that for a moment he'd allowed himself to forget how much was between them.

And the way she'd felt in his arms.

How could he have forgotten how right it felt to hold her?

He shook his head as he pulled into the parking lot of Autumn Haven Assisted Living Facility. He hadn't forgotten. He'd just chosen not to remember. Once he'd broken up with Lauren, once she'd refused his apology and arrogant offer of friendship, he'd pushed her out of his mind and heart with the same ruthlessness with which he'd forced her out of his life. A month later, he'd met Donna. Blond. Beautiful. Driven. Everything he'd imagined he'd wanted. There'd been no question they would date, marry, have a life together. Perhaps if they'd talked a little more about what that life would be, there wouldn't have been as much tension and disappointment for both of them. Much as Seth had admired his wife's drive and focus, he'd been appalled by her inability to bond with their often-sick child. Perhaps that would have changed if Donna had lived.

"You're early, Seth." The raspy voice belonged to lifetime smoker and curmudgeon, Matt Webber. A former professor at Magnolia College, he'd retired ten years ago and had recently moved into Autumn Haven.

Seth crossed the small porch that shaded the entry of Matt's condo and smiled. "I'm not the only one. Aren't you usually doing some kind of basket-weaving class about now?"

"Basket weaving is for sissies. I'm doing ceramics. Got myself a nice bowl almost ready to fire."

"And about twenty women all anxious to help you figure out how to do it."

"Shh." Matt glanced around. "Wouldn't want the other singles to hear that."

"Good point. So, do you want to take care of business out here, or inside?"

"Here's fine. Let me get us some sweet tea and then we'll go over the changes I want you to make in my will."

Seth forced himself not to glance at his watch. One thing he'd learned in the years since he'd moved to Magnolia Falls—it wasn't good to rush a meeting. Unlike in Savannah where his clients had been young, hip and always in a hurry, his clients in Magnolia Falls were mostly elderly who'd learned the true value of time. They didn't waste it, but they didn't rush it, either, and meetings could go on for much longer than the hour Seth planned. Fortunately, he had Reese to fall back on. She was always there when Jake got home from school, always willing to stay a little longer when necessary. Maybe, though, he'd been counting on her a little too much.

"What's the scowl for, boy?" Matt set a glass of tea on the table with enough force to send liquid splashing over the rim. "You're young, healthy, got a family to be proud of. Scowls are reserved for men like me. Old codgers who got no one."

"Except for twenty women vying for their attention."

"There's that." Matt smiled, sipped his own tea. "So, what's the problem?"

"No problem. Want to tell me what you called me out here for? I thought we'd gotten the details of your will ironed out last month."

"Yeah, me, too. But all this hoopla about library renovations and the body found on campus has got me thinking. Maybe leaving all my money to this place isn't what I want."

"It's your decision, Matt. You know that. Whatever you want, I'll make sure it happens."

"Good. What I'm thinking is that I want to leave half my money to Autumn Haven just like we planned. The other half I want to give to the college alumni association."

"Any stipulation on what they can use it for?"

"Nah. I worked at that college for long enough, I trust them to make good financial decisions."

Seth jotted down some notes. "That sounds good to me. Anything else?"

"Not unless you can fix me up with a date while you're getting all that paperwork ready."

"Weren't you at the fund-raiser dinner last week with Janice Montgomery?"

"Sure was, but we're not exclusive."

"Does she know that?"

"Of course she does." Matt humphed and lifted his tea for a sip. His hands were tan, speckled with age spots, and trembling enough for Seth to notice.

He settled back in his seat, suddenly not as anxious to finish and be on his way. Time had limits. Lives had endings. It was a blessing and a burden to know so many who were getting so close to theirs. "Did you enjoy the evening?"

"Not as much as I wanted to. Too much talk of dead people for my peace of mind."

"You mean the body that was found?"

"That and other deaths. You probably don't remember that young boy. Sean? Scott? Used to play basketball?"

"Scott Winters?" He'd been a star basketball player until he was injured in the play-offs.

"Died of alcohol poisoning they said. I always wondered, though. That was one good kid. Then there was Adam Kessler's death. An accident they said."

"Scott did die from alcohol poisoning and Adam's death *was* an accident." A tragic boating accident. One that Seth had always felt could have been prevented. Of course, he hadn't been there and had only known what was written in the newspaper and reported to Seth by friends.

"So was the wreck that nearly killed the Buchanan kid. The one who writes comic books now. He never was the same. Seems like a lot of tragedy happening around the same time."

"Not really, Matt. Those incidents were pretty spread out. If they'd had something to do with each other the police would have made the connection."

"Never said they were connected. Just said I was tired of hearing about them. Bad vibes. Bad luck. Curses.

Everyone around this place is talking about how Magnolia College has one of those things. Bunch of hogwash."

"I couldn't agree more." Though he had to admit, he was intrigued. He'd never thought about the string of incidents together, but now that he had he couldn't stop wondering. Was there any connection between the things Matt had mentioned? Did those things have anything to do with the e-mail Lauren had received? And could there be some connection between the long-ago incidents and Ellen's disappearance?

They were questions he was still asking himself as he pulled out of Autumn Haven's parking lot. He'd been wanting to find his sister for years, praying that she was all right, hoping that eventually she'd get in touch. He'd hired a private investigator, contacted old high school friends, none had been able to give him information on Ellen's location. Part of the problem was his own distance from his sister's college life. Older by more than six years, Ellen had seemed an exotic enigma to Seth. She'd loved him, had always been willing to lend a hand with homework, give advice about girls and dating, but her volatile personality had often caused more stress than comfort in their childhood home. After she'd graduated from Magnolia College, she'd seldom returned home, seldom made contact with Seth or his parents, and had often disappeared for months at a time. Still, there'd always been a connection between sister and brother, and Seth had attended Magnolia College partially because Ellen had thought it was right for him.

He missed her. Pure and simple. And he was worried.

If he could figure out who she'd hung out with during her years at the school, if he could contact some of those people, maybe he could find her. Up until now, he hadn't had access to alumni information, but with Lauren and her friends' new Web site, he could easily e-mail people who posted information and had graduated the same year as Ellen. Maybe one of them would remember her. Maybe one of them *knew* her.

He needed to call Lauren, discuss things with her, see what she thought.

At least that's what he would have done when they were in high school. Maybe even during his first couple of years at college. It was not what he should be doing now.

Years had passed. He'd changed. Lauren had changed. Maybe there was room for a phone call, a discussion. Maybe even something more. Who knew what God had planned? Seth didn't, and, he decided as he reached for his cell phone, there was no way he planned to put limits on the possibilities.

Lauren stepped out of the police station, inhaled air thick with moisture. There'd be rain tonight. Maybe even a storm. That was fine with her. She'd always loved rain—the soft sound of water splashing onto earth, the heavy moisture in the air, the deep green of the leaves against the gray sky. Tonight would be a perfect time to be locked inside the carriage house, a good book in one hand, a cup of tea in the other. Maybe she'd bake something. Brownies? She could even make them gluten-free and bring them over to Jake.

Scratch that.

She'd make them double-chocolate and give them to Dee.

Her cell phone rang as she got into her car, and she grabbed it. "Hello?"

"Lauren. It's Seth."

As if he had to tell her. As if she didn't recognize his voice the minute he spoke. "What's up?"

"I just had an interesting conversation with a retired Magnolia College professor. It made me think about that e-mail you received last night."

"How so?"

"He mentioned a couple of things that happened during the years we were at college. Adam Kessler's death. Scott Winter's death. The accident that injured Parker Buchanan."

"I remember. They were horrible tragedies, but I haven't really thought about any of them in years."

"Me, neither, but this professor mentioned that they'd all happened in the years preceding the first library renovations."

"You mean before a body ended up beneath the library sidewalk."

"That's exactly what I mean."

"And?"

"I don't know, but it makes me wonder if things at Magnolia College were different than we perceived them to be. Maybe there was more going on there than we thought."

"Like murder?" She couldn't conceive of it, didn't even want to think about it.

"The police will know soon enough, Lola, but if that woman *was* murdered, it happened the year you graduated. Someone attending college at the time must know what happened and why."

"I'm sure the police will investigate."

"I'm sure they will, too, but not as quickly as I plan to."

"You plan to investigate?" That didn't sound smart. Not if there really was a murderer wandering around town.

"Not in the same way the police will. I just want to ask a few questions, find out if there were whispers and rumors that I'm not aware of."

"Seth, what you're doing could be dangerous. If that woman was murdered and you start digging into the past—"

"If that woman was Ellen, I can't *not* dig into the past."

"But you don't know that it is. All you know is that you haven't heard from your sister in ten years. That doesn't mean she's been buried beneath a sidewalk all this time." Just the thought was appalling, and Lauren's heart raced with it.

"You're right, but I need to know one way or the other."

"What can I do to help?"

He was quiet for a moment, and when he spoke his words were filled with a thousand memories. "Thanks for offering. All I need is what I already asked. Read the guest book entries. Let me know if my sister contacts you or if you get any more strange e-mails."

"All right. Anything else?"

"Come by my house for dinner tomorrow night. We'll compare notes. See if we can come up with a list of people who were at Magnolia College ten years ago and who haven't been heard from since."

"My friends and I have already done that."

"Students *and* employees?"

"Just students."

"So, let's see who else we can come up with."

She almost said yes. Almost slipped right back into old habits. Fortunately, sanity prevailed. "I think it would be better not to."

"Because you're afraid to spend more time with me?"

"I don't *want* to spend more time with you."

"Am I that bad as company?"

He was too good as company, his presence bringing back memories Lauren knew were better not dwelled on. "You're part of my past, Seth. I want to keep you there."

"I'm not sure that's going to be possible, Lola."

"I'm not sure you have a choice."

He chuckled, the warmth of it seeping into her heart. "I'm not sure you do, either."

Before she could respond, he hung up.

He was wrong, of course. She did have a choice. Seth was not going to become a part of her life again.

Become part of it? He already was *part of it.*

Lauren frowned. Maybe he was right, maybe there wasn't any way to keep her distance from Seth while she was in town, but she wouldn't be here long. Once she got back to Savannah things would get back to normal. *She* would get back to normal. No more thoughts of Seth. No more dwelling on dreams that hadn't been fulfilled. After all, she had a good life. No, a great life. Friends. Family. Work. God had blessed her. She needed to be happy with that. She *was* happy with that.

So why did the life she'd created in Savannah suddenly feel more empty than full?

Because she was tired, that's why. Nothing more or less than that. As soon as she got a good night's sleep and a few days off, she'd feel a hundred times better about everything in her life. Including Seth and all the memories he'd resurrected.

THIRTEEN

Rain brought memories. Good ones. Not so good ones. It also made doing what needed to be done easier. It covered tracks, loosened soil, masked sounds. Those things were important. So was waiting for the right time.

It was not the right time.

The wee hours of the morning, the moments that were darkest, when moon and stars had faded but the sun had yet to begin its ascent. Most people would be sleeping now, enjoying their dreams or fighting their nightmares.

Most people, but not her.

Lights still shone from the carriage house, spilling out onto the manicured lawn, lightening the storm-darkened night and casting shadows and brightness that could hide or reveal. Moving closer would require stealth and guts. Those weren't a problem. It would be easy enough to get inside the little house. A knock on the door, a quiet conversation, a quick thrust of a knife and it could all be over, but that wasn't the plan.

For now, following the plan was vital. Keeping hidden. Keeping quiet. Following the rules. Waiting for the right time. Eventually everything would blow over. People would forget as they had before. Life would go on.

For some.

Two o'clock in the morning.

She was supposed to be sleeping. That was the plan. Sleep. Vacation. Feel better about everything. Instead, Lauren paced the carriage house living room, rain splashing against the roof, wind slapping against the windows, the scent of the curry and jasmine rice she'd made for dinner hanging in the air. Maybe it was the curry that was keeping her awake. Maybe it was the rain. Or maybe it was her ever-spinning thoughts. Whatever the case, she was awake and two cups of chamomile tea hadn't changed that.

She moved into the kitchen, pulling bowls and ingredients from the cupboards and refrigerator, not really conscious of what she was doing until yeast was proofing in a bowl by the stove and she was cracking eggs into flour. Egg bread. A nice braid of it with cinnamon, raisins, maybe a sweet glaze. Dee would love it.

Lauren would love it. A thick slice with a hot cup of coffee. Perfect. Her stomach rumbled just thinking about it.

The phone rang as she gently kneaded raisins into soft dough, and she grabbed it, not thinking about the time, her sticky flour-covered fingers or the trouble that seemed to be following her since the fund-raiser dinner. Not thinking about anything but the yeasty aroma of bread, the easy rhythm of kneading.

"Hello?"

Silence. A deep breath, raspy and strange.

A chill shot up Lauren's spine, and she turned away

from the dough, her pulse sludging through her veins and echoing hollowly in her ears. "Hello? Is someone there?"

"Go home, Lauren Owens." The words, like the breath, sounded raspy and thick. Not male. Not female. A disembodied sound that could have come from anyone and from anywhere.

"Who is this?"

"Someone who would hate to see anything happen to you."

"What are you talking about?" She glanced at the caller ID. *Caller unknown.*

"You're sticking your nose into things you shouldn't. That can be dangerous."

"Explain what you mean and maybe I'll understand what the problem is."

"There won't be a problem if you do what you're told and go home." The phone clicked, the line dying.

A crank call.

No. A threat.

Lauren glanced at the clock, jotted down the time, her hands shaking as she hurried across the room to check the new security system. It was on. The doors were locked. She was safe.

She didn't feel safe, though, and only the thought of her sister crossing the darkened yard to come stay with her kept Lauren from picking up the phone and calling Dee.

Time slowed, the heavy rain slashing against the window, every creak, every groan making Lauren's nerves jump. It was at times like these that she regretted not spending more time pursuing a relationship. If she had, maybe she'd have a husband to peer out the windows for her, check to make sure no one was lurking outside.

"You don't need a man to do that. You're an independent, confident woman who knows that no one is outside the windows trying to see in. Just go over there and take a look." Her words sounded hollow, but Lauren moved forward anyway. Fear crawled up her spine, lodged in her skull, beat a horrifying warning in the slushing pulse of her racing heart. When she'd been a kid, she'd given in to it. It had been Dee who'd opened closet doors to search for monsters, who'd checked under beds for bogeymen, who'd laughed at the playground bully. Later, Seth had stepped in. Always there to check for danger and to face it. Spiders. Mice. Dark shadows. He'd never laughed at Lauren or downplayed her worries. Strong, seemingly fearless, he'd been a knight in shining armor to her damsel in distress.

Too bad he hadn't bought into the happily-ever-after idea.

Actually, he had. Just not with her.

In the end, it was for the best.

Nowadays Lauren faced spiders, mice and dark shadows herself. And if something was lurking outside, she'd face that, too. Heart in her throat, she grabbed the heavy drapes and tugged them back. Beyond the window, the world was black onyx, glistening and dark. Light from the window spread out across the lawn, touching deep shadows and hulking shapes, making more mysteries out of the gloom. Anything could be hiding there. *Anyone* could be hiding there.

"No one is, Lord. I know that. I also know that You're in control. Help me trust that You're looking out for me."

The simple prayer was enough to calm Lauren's nerves. Knights rode off into the sunset and never returned, but

God was constant and steady, true and sure. When others abandoned, He stayed close. When others turned away, He remained. That was a truth more powerful than fear, a reality more compelling than the wildest imaginings. That was what Lauren had clung to in the weeks and months following Seth's desertion. It was one she still clung to.

She let the curtains drop and retreated back into the kitchen, finishing the sweet bread by rote, covering it with a cloth to let it rise, grabbing her Bible and sinking onto the love seat while time passed and dawn slowly stole away the night.

By seven o'clock, the sun had crested the stand of trees beyond Dee's property line and Lauren had baked two loaves of raisin bread, a batch of oatmeal cookies and a batch of gluten-free brownies. The first two were for her sister, the last should be, too, but that wasn't why Lauren had baked them. After a sleepless night, she could at least admit that.

She'd made the brownies for Jake.

Sad, but true. No matter how much she might want to keep Seth out of her life, she couldn't forget his son's excitement at the prospect of having kid-friendly food to share with his friends. It was tough enough being a ten-year-old kid. Being different only made it worse. For Lauren it had been her bookish intelligence that had set her apart. For Jake it was his food allergies. The results were the same—a chasm between self and classmates that seemed almost impossible to forge. Maybe a few more brownies would help bridge that gap for Jake. They wouldn't hurt anyway.

She showered quickly, throwing on faded jeans and a

soft sweater, scraping still-wet hair into a low ponytail and putting the baked goods in two bags. She carried those and her laptop out into the early morning. The rain had stopped, but moisture was thick in the air, the trees and grass shimmering with reflected sunlight. As Lauren rounded the side of the house, the door opened and Dee appeared, her dark suit emphasizing her slim figure, her hair pulled away from her perfectly made-up face. She smiled as she caught sight of Lauren, her eyes dancing with humor. "For someone who's on vacation, you sure are up early."

"Up? I never slept." Lauren passed one of the bags to her sister. "I made some sweet bread."

"With raisins?"

"And glaze. There's oatmeal cookies in there, too."

"Keep it up and I'll be ten pounds heavier by the time you go home." Dee peered into the bag, inhaling deeply.

"That's why I packed it up and brought it out now. I figured you can bring it to work and share it."

"Share? We'll see." Dee pulled open her car door and set the bag inside. "So, what kept you baking all night? You're still worried about what happened the other night?"

"Partly that. Partly other things."

"Like?"

"The past. Seth mentioned some of the things that happened when we were at Magnolia College. Adam Kessler's death. Scott's."

"That was ten years ago, Lauren. You can't get yourself upset about it now."

"I'm not. It just seems odd. So many things going wrong in such a short period of time."

"Two things isn't a lot."

"Three, if you count the body buried beneath the sidewalk. Four, if you count Parker Buchanan's accident."

"I don't. Each has nothing to do with the others."

"Seth's sister, Ellen, is missing, too. He hasn't seen her for ten years."

"Ellen was always a free spirit. Even when she lived at home she wasn't there much. I can remember you coming home from the Chartrands' saying how glad you were we didn't have huge fights with our parents the way Ellen did with hers."

"I know, but—"

"Lauren, you worry too much. Look up the stats for any university. I guarantee you'll find a list of accidents and incidents that puts Magnolia College's to shame. Things happen. Bad things. Good things. We saw a lot of both while we were in college. It was normal. Not sinister."

"No? Well the phone call I got at two this morning was."

"What phone call?" Dee's eyes went dark with worry, and she rubbed a hand against the back of her neck.

"Someone wants me to go home and stop sticking my nose into other people's business."

"Did you call the police?"

"Not yet. I figured I'd contact them after the sun came up."

"I wish you hadn't waited." ·

"There was nothing the police could do. It wasn't like someone was trying to break down the door to get to me."

"Still…" Dee closed the car door, her face pale beneath her makeup. "Maybe I'd better stay home and go to the police with you. First the vandalism, then that strange e-mail, now a threatening call. I don't like it."

"I don't, either, but that doesn't mean you've got to escort me to the police." Lauren smiled, hoping her fatigue and worry weren't as evident on her face as they were in her mind.

"I won't be escorting you. I'll just be coming along for the ride."

"Like you did when we were kids and Mom and Dad made me admit to the principal that I'd cut school on senior hook day?"

"Something like that." Dee smiled, some of her worry easing.

"I appreciate it, Dee, but I'm not a kid anymore. I can handle this on my own. Besides, I'm sure you've got a hundred meetings today."

"Just two, but they *are* important." She hesitated, shrugged. "All right. I'll go to work. You go to the police, but if anything else happens call me."

"What else could happen?"

"I don't know. That's what I'm worried about." Dee got into her car, started the engine. "Be careful."

"You, too." Lauren waved as her sister drove away, a hard knot of unease in her stomach.

Maybe Dee was right. Maybe the past had nothing to do with what was happening now, but Lauren couldn't help thinking that the library renovations that had uncovered the body had also uncovered something violent and ugly. Something that would be better off hidden.

Too late now.

Whatever had happened in the past would soon come to light. Lauren only prayed that no one else would suffer as the poor woman who'd died ten years ago had.

FOURTEEN

He was running late again. Seth grabbed his briefcase, glanced at his watch and decided not to look at it again. Eight-fifteen. The electricity was still out thanks to last night's storm, but at least Jake was up and moving.

"Come on, kid. You've already missed the bus. If we leave now you'll only be a few minutes late to school."

"Coming." Jake hurried down the stairs, his strawberry hair tousled.

"Did you comb your hair?"

"Yeah."

"Maybe you should do it again in the car."

"Why? Does it look bad?" Jake's cheeks heated, and Seth wished he'd kept his mouth shut. Knowing his son, Jake would be self-conscious about his hair for the rest of the day.

"It looks great, but a little more combing won't hurt."

"Okay. I'll get the comb."

Seth bit back a sigh as his son ran back up the stairs. Two more minutes passed. Three. "Jake! We've got to go."

"I wet my hair down. Does it look better?" This time, Jake's hair was plastered to his head. Eventually it would dry, so Seth decided to let the subject go.

"Yep. Grab your backpack. I'm working late tonight, so Reese is going to feed you dinner and get you into bed."

"I'm ten. I can get myself into bed."

"I'll make sure I tell her that." Seth smiled as he ushered his son outside. The rain had passed a few hours ago, and watery sunlight poured onto the grass as they moved toward the car. It was going to be a beautiful day. Maybe he'd manage to finish work earlier than he thought, and he and Jake would have time for a bike ride.

"Hey, isn't that Miss Lauren's car?"

"Where?"

"Coming toward us. There. The yellow Mustang."

Sure enough, Lauren's vintage Mustang was moving toward them. Slowly. As if she were hoping they'd be gone before she arrived. Unfortunately for her, there was no way he planned to leave before he found out why she was driving by his house so early in the morning.

He watched as she pulled up in front of the house and got out of the car. Her hair was pulled back from a face that was several shades too pale, her eyes deeply shadowed and filled with anxiety.

"What's wrong?" He strode toward her, the urge to help, to protect, to make sure she was okay filling him the way it had when she'd been a timid teenager and anxious young woman.

"Nothing." Her smile was too bright, but she lifted a plastic bag and held it out to him. "I made some brownies and thought I'd leave them on your porch. I figured you'd both be gone by now."

"You mean you were *hoping* we'd be gone," Seth whispered into her ear as he took her elbow and started back toward Jake.

"That, too." She smiled again. "Good morning, Jake."

"Good morning. Are there brownies in that bag?"

"Jake—"

Lauren's laughter interrupted his warning, and Seth decided not to reprimand his son after all. At least when she was laughing Lauren didn't look so worn-out and anxious. "How'd you know?"

"I can smell the chocolate."

Seth thought what his son was smelling was Lauren— that sweet, wholesome scent that had always seemed to cling to her. Chocolate. Vanilla. Comfort on a difficult day.

"I did some baking last night. While I was at it I made the brownies. I thought you might like to share them with friends after school. Since you're still here, maybe you can bring them to school instead."

"That would be great. Thanks!" To Seth's surprise, Jake threw his arms around Lauren's waist.

She hugged him back, her dark ponytail sliding over her shoulder as she smiled down into his face. "You're welcome. Did you and your friends enjoy the last batch I made?"

"You bet. Some of my friends were asking if you could make chocolate chip cookies."

"Jacob Andrew, don't even go there." Seth put a hand on Jake's shoulder, stopping his son before he could ask Lauren to do more than she already had.

"It's okay." Lauren met his eyes, her soft smile pulling him in as it always had. "It doesn't take long to make a batch of cookies."

"Maybe not, but you've already done plenty." And she looked exhausted. "This is your vacation. Enjoy it."

"I enjoy baking, so a few cookies won't be a big deal." She stepped back toward her car. "I'd better let you two get on with your day."

"And we'd better let you get on with yours. Hop in the car, Jake."

As his son climbed in and closed the car door, Seth followed Lauren to the Mustang. "You look tired."

"Thanks. That's just what every woman wants a man to say to her."

"Beautiful, but tired." He brushed a long strand of hair from her cheek, looking into her eyes, trying to read whatever secret she was hiding. "What's going on?"

"Just…" She shrugged, moving away from his hand. "It was a long night."

"Tell me."

"Someone called around two this morning and said I should go back home. That he'd hate for something to happen to me."

Seth tensed at her words, adrenaline pumping through him at the thought of someone threatening Lauren. "Did you call the police?"

"I'm going into the station to make a report now."

"You okay?"

"Fine. Just wondering why someone has got a problem with me being here."

"Who have you seen since you've been in town?"

"Who haven't I seen? I was at the fund-raiser dinner, remember?" She sighed, smoothed a hand over the curls that were beginning to escape her ponytail. "I really need to go. Tell Jake I'm going to make those cookies for him."

She started to get in the car, but he put a hand on her arm, holding her in place. "Let me help, Lola. I'll go to the police with you, see if we can get a patrol car at your sister's house for the next few nights."

For just a moment she looked as though she'd agree, her expression soft, open, speaking to him of fear and anxiety and a longing that made him want to pull her into his arms. Then she tugged against his hold and slid into her car. "I appreciate the offer, but I'd better take care of things myself."

Let her go. Take your son to school. Get on with your day.

That's what he *should* do, but it wasn't what he was going to do. What he was going to do was drop Jake off, cancel his first appointment and head over to the police station. Lauren might not want him to be there, but he'd never been one to hesitate when he thought what he was doing was right. *This* was right. For now, that was what mattered.

It took less time at the police station than Lauren thought it would. Detective Anderson listened to her story, assured her that he'd do what he could to trace the call, informed her that they'd had no luck locating the origins of the guest book entry she'd received and cautioned her to stay out of any investigation involving Magnolia College alumni. One body, he'd said, was enough.

Lauren couldn't agree more, but the Web site wasn't an investigation. It was a way of assuring herself that people she cared about were alive and well. That was something she didn't plan to give up.

Bright sunshine nearly blinded her as she stepped out

of the police station, the heat of it seeping through her sweater and easing the chill that had been dogging her for the past few hours.

"How'd it go?"

The voice was so unexpected, Lauren whirled toward it, nearly losing her balance as she faced Seth. He looked good, thick hair falling over his forehead, stubble covering his jaw as if he hadn't had time to shave, green eyes bright against tanned skin. So similar to what she remembered, but so different. "What are you doing here?"

"Waiting for you."

"You know that's not what I mean."

"Did you expect me to hear about what happened to you and go on with my day?"

"Yes."

"I think you know me better than that."

"*Knew* you better than that. A lifetime ago." She leaned a shoulder against the brick wall of the building, fatigue dragging her down.

"Don't kid yourself, Lola. Ten years, twenty, a lifetime, I don't think any amount of time can completely wipe out what we had."

She laughed, the sound forced, her heart thudding painfully in her chest. "Seth, what we had died the night you told me I was too boring and predictable to fit into the exciting life you had planned."

"That isn't what I said."

"No, but it's what you meant."

"Maybe." He raked a hand through his hair, his gaze fixed on some distant point. Some distant time. "But it wasn't what I felt."

"Of course it was. What was it you said to me? 'Women are like cars. Some are station wagons. Some are sports cars. Both are nice cars, but a guy who wants to drive fast and go far is never going to be happy with a station wagon.'"

"Did I really say that?" His lips twitched, and Lauren couldn't stop her own smile.

"I'm afraid so."

"I was even more of an arrogant jerk than I remembered."

"Yeah. You were." But not at first, and standing here talking to him was reminding Lauren of what she'd loved most about Seth—his willingness to listen, his ability to hear what she was saying even when she couldn't put it into words that made sense. Where others had overlooked the quiet, rather mousy Owens sister, Seth had not just noticed, but paid attention to her, cherished her, loved her.

For a while anyway.

Lauren straightened. "I'd better go."

"Why?"

"Because I can't stand around the police station all day." She started back toward her car, and Seth fell into step beside her.

"How about going to the Half Joe with me? We can grab some coffee and something to eat."

The Half Joe was exactly where she'd been planning to go. Alone. "I'm sure you've got better things to do with your time."

"Nothing that can't wait." He smiled, his eyes crinkling at the corners. "Come on, Lola. It's just coffee. That's all. I promise."

Promise? The words rang through her mind, echoing a distant memory.

"I love you, Lola." His eyes were so green, so filled with assurance, Lauren felt her heart swell with it.

"Forever?"

"Of course, forever."

"Even when we're both gray-haired and wrinkled?"

"Even then." He pressed his lips to hers, the joy of the contact spearing through her.

"You promise?"

He kissed his way from her lips to her ear, whispering the words she wanted so desperately to believe. *"I promise."*

"Lola? How about it?"

Promises. She didn't believe them, but she didn't need to anymore. What she did need was a cup of coffee. Whether or not she should have that coffee with Seth was something she couldn't quite decide. "I guess it can't hurt."

"Great. Your car, or mine?" He smiled again, and this time there was something in his eyes she knew only too well. Interest. Attraction. Chemistry. They'd made her heart beat faster when she was a kid. Now she was immune.

Sure she was.

She frowned and turned away, pulling open the door of the Mustang. "Both. I've got some errands to run later."

"Sounds good. I'll meet you there." He walked away, his stride as confident and sure as it had always been, his shoulders a little broader, his hair a little shorter, and Lauren felt something stir to life inside her, something she was sure had died a long time ago. Her heart jumped with it, her mind rebelling.

She was *not* attracted to Seth.

If she were, she wouldn't have agreed to have coffee

with him. What she was feeling was nothing more than fatigue, or hunger, or both.

She kept telling herself that as she climbed into the Mustang and headed for the Half Joe. Anything else was unacceptable. Anything else was just too frightening to contemplate. Anything else would cause her more trouble and heartache than she ever wanted to experience again.

You know that, Lord, so I'm giving this over to you. I've got too many other things to think about, so I'm just going to go have a cup of coffee with an old friend and let You worry about everything else.

At least that's what she'd try to do.

Only time would tell if she'd be successful.

FIFTEEN

Lauren didn't wait for Seth to pull into the parking lot before she made her way inside. That would have seemed too much like waiting for a date, and this wasn't a date. It was coffee. Something she desperately needed.

As always, the coffee shop buzzed with college students, and Lauren wove her way through the crowd until she found two empty chairs.

"I see you found a spot." Seth appeared at her side, his gaze searching hers.

Maybe he was surprised that she'd agreed to have coffee with him. *She* certainly was. "I think these are the only seats left in the place."

"Then stay here and guard them while I go grab the coffee. What else do you want? A Danish? Doughnut? Muffin?"

"Just get your own, and I'll go up after you."

"That seems like a waste of time and effort."

"Not to me."

"We could argue about it. Or I could just do what I'm planning to and you could decide to be happy about it."

Lauren shook her head, laughing a little as she settled into an overstuffed chair. "Fine. Have it your way. I'll take a coffee and a cinnamon roll. And maybe a cheese Danish if they've got them."

"Both?" A slow smile spread across his hard face, his eyes sparkling with amusement.

"Yes. Why?"

"I thought maybe you'd become one of those calorie-conscious women who picks at her food."

"Nope. I still love to eat and I still love to cook. Those things haven't changed."

"Your style of cooking has. No more deep-fried Southern fare."

"That depends on the client. Most people I work with want healthier menus. I try to accommodate that without giving up flavor. Comfort food without all the fat."

"It works. Jake has enjoyed every one of the meals you cooked. I have, too."

"I'm glad." Lauren brushed curls away from her face and wondered what else she was supposed to say.

Should having coffee with an old friend be so awkward? Probably not, but, then, Seth wasn't really an old friend.

"I'll be back in a minute." He saved her from further comment by moving away, weaving through the crowd, a few inches taller than most of the other patrons. Older than them, too. Confident, but not cocky the way he'd been when he'd been attending Magnolia College.

What had his life been like during the past few years? Lauren had heard about his marriage, his wife, her death, but she didn't know the details, or the truth. She hadn't thought she wanted to. Seeing Seth again, watching him with his son, made her wonder, though. All his big dreams about a career in criminal law, world travel, financial success, fast boats, fast cars. Had he willingly put them aside, or had they drifted into the background after his marriage?

She forced her mind away from the questions, opening her laptop and turning it on. She had plenty of other things she could do besides thinking about a man who'd once compared her to a station wagon.

"You look irritated." He handed her a cup of coffee and set a fragrant cinnamon roll and a flaky Danish on the little table in front of her. "You've got a frown line right here." His finger skimmed the place between her brows, spreading warmth in its wake.

Lauren's cheeks heated, her heart skipped, her stomach flipped, and she knew she'd made a big mistake agreeing to have coffee with Seth.

Keep the conversation neutral. Keep her feelings in check. Pretend she was dealing with a client. Simple. Easy. Lauren took a deep breath. A client. She could do that. "I'm not irritated, and for the record, I do not have a frown line."

"Don't worry, Lola. It's only noticeable when you scowl." The laughter in his voice tempted her to look up, meet his eyes, see the amused affection she knew would be there.

Like old times. Other days.

She kept her eyes fixed on the computer screen, refusing to be drawn into Seth's easy charm and good humor. "Keep it up, Seth. You're doing a great job of reminding me of why I slammed the door in your face after you apologized for breaking up with me."

"In my face? More like on my face."

"I told you to back up."

"I know, but I didn't believe you were actually going to shut me out."

"I wasn't the one who did the shutting out." She pulled up her e-mail in-box, took a sip of coffee and was disgusted to see that her hand was trembling.

"You're right." Laughter had faded from his voice and he cupped her chin, urging her to look up, to meet his eyes. "I regretted hurting you as soon as it happened. If I could have taken back the words, made things right between us, I would have."

"But you couldn't. What we had was too broken to be mended." She smiled, her mouth dry, her nerves alive with something she refused to name. "I thought we came here for coffee. If we're going to talk about the past, maybe I should go."

"Stay." His hand slipped away. "No more talk about the past. I promise."

"And no more promises."

"If that's what you want."

"It is."

He leaned back in his chair, took a bite of what looked like a double chocolate muffin, his gaze touching Lauren's hair, her cheeks, her lips.

Her skin heated beneath his scrutiny, and she fidgeted, swiping a napkin across her mouth. "Is there something on my face?"

"Nope, just thinking."

"About?"

"The past, but I told you I wouldn't talk about it. So, why don't you tell me what you're working on?" He gestured to the computer and Lauren turned it in his direction. Anything to focus his attention away from her.

"The Web site. We've got a couple dozen guest book

entries already posted, and there are ten more here I need to read through and approve."

"Mind if I take a look?"

"Go ahead."

He slid the laptop out of her hands, his knuckles brushing her thigh, his shoulder leaning into hers, stealing her space. Her breath.

Then he straightened, the laptop on his knees, his head bent over the screen, and the world righted again. "Look, this one is from someone who graduated the same year as Ellen."

"Twila Morton. Do you recognize the name?"

"Maybe. I remember that Ellen had a good friend with an unusual name. I was too into my own world to notice much more about it than that."

"She's left her e-mail address. You can contact her and find out if she knows your sister." Lauren skimmed the next entry, excitement stealing some of her fatigue as she read the name. "There's one from Gavin Fisher and one from Deborah Michaels. I can't wait to tell the others that she's okay. She had such big dreams and hopes. She wanted to change the world." Lauren smiled as she remembered the quiet young woman.

"She says she's working for the Red Cross."

"That fits. Anyone else we know?" She leaned close, forgetting for a moment that she should keep her distance, enjoying, just for a second, the feeling of camaraderie, of shared goals, of common interests.

"Seth! What are you doing here? I thought you had meetings all day." The feminine voice was like a splash of ice water on a hot day.

Lauren jerked up and away from Seth, her eyes meeting Reese's, her cheeks burning.

Which was ridiculous. She had nothing to be embarrassed about.

"I do, but I postponed my earliest until tomorrow." Seth's explanation didn't seem to appease Reese.

She frowned. Or maybe it was more of a pout. "If you'd canceled this evening's meeting instead, we could have had dinner together."

Okay. Lauren was done with this. She felt like a voyeur watching some dreadful soap opera play out. "If you two will excuse me. I've got to head out."

"I'll walk out with you." Seth stood, handing her the laptop.

"That's okay, I can find my own way out. Nice seeing you again, Reese. Thanks for the coffee, Seth." She hurried away, knowing it was for the best. She'd been a little too relaxed with Seth, a little too eager to fall back into old habits of sharing and discussion.

"You left before you could finish eating."

Lauren should have known Seth would follow her. He'd always been tenacious. When he'd made up his mind to pursue something, nothing could stand in his way. Apparently, that hadn't changed.

She turned to face him, steeling herself against the intensity of his gaze and the curiosity she saw there. "I guess I wasn't as hungry as I thought."

"Then take them with you for later." He passed her the cinnamon roll and Danish wrapped in napkins. "You really didn't have to run off, Lola. Reese was just grabbing coffee before heading back to campus."

"I wasn't running."

"Sure you were. I'm just not sure why."

"I don't like being a third wheel."

"A third wheel? You don't think Reese and I..." His voice trailed off, and he chuckled. "I'm thirty-three. A girl Reese's age holds absolutely no interest for me."

"She's not a girl, and I've known plenty of men your age who wouldn't mind dating a college student, and some who actually prefer it."

"Yeah, well I don't. Twenty-something is fine for twenty-somethings. I prefer women who are a little more mature, a little more settled, a little more like—"

"From what Reese said, it sounds like you've got a busy day ahead. I'd better head out and let you get on with it." She cut him off before he could finish, sliding into her car and pulling the door shut.

He stood in the parking lot and watched her go. Lauren didn't have to glance in the rearview mirror to know it. It's what he'd always done, waiting until she was out of sight before turning away, taking that extra minute for a final wave. What he'd always done until he'd decided to step out of her life completely.

And now he was back in it.

Lauren wasn't sure how she felt about that. She knew how she *should* feel. Indifferent. Unaffected. Unfortunately, knowing how she should feel wasn't helping her feel that way. Instead, she was confused. In the past, she'd imagined seeing Seth again, but imagining had done little to prepare her for the reality, or for the fact that despite time, heartache and anger, she was still attracted to him.

That couldn't be good.

It wasn't good, but Lauren wasn't sure there was anything she could do about it. She grabbed the Danish, took a bite. Food wouldn't help, but it would fill her stomach. At least that was something she could control. She'd have to leave everything else in God's hands.

SIXTEEN

Sunday morning arrived in shades of orange and purple, the sun creeping over the trees as Lauren sipped coffee and stared out the window. The last two days had been relaxing and uneventful. Exactly what she'd been telling herself she wanted and needed. The problem was, she was used to a busy schedule, hectic weekdays, weekends spent catching up on all the things that she put on hold during the workweek. Two days of doing nothing had proven what she'd long suspected—vacationing was hard work.

Of course, it might be a whole lot easier if she weren't spending so much time thinking about not thinking about Seth. She grimaced and moved away from the window. Despite all her efforts to keep him out of her head, Seth had taken up residence there and no amount of self-talk, lectures or warnings seemed able to dislodge him. On the upside, she hadn't received any more crank calls or strange guest book entries. That had to count for something.

She grabbed clothes from her room, took a quick shower and dried her hair, pulling out the curls and straightening them with a flatiron. Makeup, heels, a spritz of perfume and she was ready to leave. Too bad it wasn't time to go.

She paced across the room, staring out the window again, her stomach churning and twisting with nerves and anxiety. In the past few years, she'd been to France, to Italy, to Spain, to Thailand, to Mexico. She'd crisscrossed the United States conducting workshops on allergen-free cooking. She'd forced herself to become more like Dee— confident, at ease in the spotlight, ready to take center stage—and after a while, that self-assured, professional persona had begun to fit.

So why be nervous today? It wasn't as if she was presenting a cooking technique at a premier culinary institute. She was going to church, sitting in a pew, listening to a sermon. There was nothing difficult or scary about that. Except that she'd felt a stirring of jealousy when Reese had approached Seth at the Half Joe.

Jealousy.

She hated to even think the word when it came to her feelings for Seth.

"Just remember how fickle he is. Just remember that his words are smooth as honey when he's making promises and sharp as a sword when he's saying good-bye. That's all you need to do, and you'll be fine." She muttered the reminder as she grabbed her purse, pulled a bag of gluten-free cookies and a plastic container of gluten-free brownies from the cupboard and headed to church.

The parking lot was nearly empty when she arrived, but the double doors were opened, inviting those who passed to enter. Lauren's heels clicked against the pavement as she moved across the parking lot, the sound echoing in the morning air. No, not quite echoing. There was something off about the beat and rhythm, something not quite hers. She glanced over her shoulder, expecting to see another parishioner heading for the church, but no one was there.

A soft breeze rustled the shrubs that lined the church building, carrying the scent of lilac and newly cut grass with it. Carrying something else. Something that was waiting to pounce.

Lauren's pulse jumped, the hair on the back of her neck standing on end. She inhaled again, but whatever she'd thought she'd sensed was gone. Still, the morning seemed darker, the sunlight dimmed. As if a shadow hovered over the parking lot.

"Good morning, Lauren!" Pastor Rogers's jovial greeting cut through the haze of Lauren's fear and pushed the world back into focus. Brightness, sunlight, the late-summer breeze. Everything normal and right. Just as it should be.

"Good morning." She hurried up the church steps, smiling at the pastor as she moved into the building. "It's a beautiful day isn't it?"

"Much too beautiful to miss out on. Have you been enjoying your vacation?"

"It's been relaxing."

"That must be what's put the color in your cheeks and the sparkle in your eye."

Actually, a very vivid imagination and fear had done that. "I'm enjoying the respite."

"Good. Good." He patted her shoulder. "We all need a break every now and again. I'm about to head into the kitchen for a cup of coffee. Care to join me?"

"Actually, I was hoping to find the kids' Sunday school class."

"We have several. What age are you looking for?"

"Ten-year-olds."

"We go by grades. Is there a particular child you're looking for?"

"Jake Chartrand. I brought some cookies and brownies for his class."

"Ah, that's right. Seth bought your chef services at the fund-raiser auction last week, didn't he? There's been quite a buzz about that."

"Have you been listening to gossip, Pastor? I'm shocked." Lauren grinned as Pastor Rogers laughed.

"What can I say? I've tried not to hear it, but it's hard to ignore when everyone makes mention of it. Apparently you and Seth were quite an item a few years back."

"Eleven years. That's more than a few."

"A few. Ten. Twenty. You get to be my age, and it all seems like the same."

"Your age? You're not that much older than me."

"I am. And I've got the gray hair to prove it. So, tell me, how has it been working with Seth and Jake?"

"Jake is a sweet kid."

"He is. Shy, though."

"Having such severe allergies doesn't help."

"And that's why you brought some special treats for him today?"

"Yes. He wants to be able to share what he thinks of as normal food with his friends."

"That makes sense. It can be tough to be different from other kids. Come on. I'll walk you down to the room." He led the way to the stairs. "Seth has insisted that we not make any adjustments to what we were doing within our program. Apparently there have been some problems at school. Other kids feel disappointed that they can't have their regular party fare when Jake is in their class."

"I imagine so."

"Seth thought it would be better if we continued to allow the children to have their regular snacks—animal crackers, chocolate cookies, that sort of thing, so as not to draw more attention to Jake. He packs something for Jake every week. Your cookies will be a special treat for everyone. Here we are." He pushed open the door to a darkened room. "You can leave the cookies here, or wait until the teacher arrives and explain. Class starts in twenty minutes."

"Thank you, Pastor."

"You're quite welcome." He smiled and disappeared back the way he'd come.

Poor Jake. Set apart from other kids by his dietary restrictions and his shy nature. It had to be tough. No wonder he was so excited by the prospect of sharing cookies and brownies with friends.

She'd planned to leave the cookies and go, but maybe she'd stick around instead. Explain things to the teacher, maybe wait to make sure the cookies were going to be used as the day's snack. Maybe even wait for Jake to arrive. He'd been so sweet the other day, his hug such a pleasant surprise. A nice kid who deserved to feel as though he fit in. The fact that his father had broken Lauren's heart was no reason to run off. Decision made, she settled into a chair, put her feet up on another one and waited.

Lauren Owens was as predictable as the sunrise. Coffee in the morning. A walk in the afternoon. Dinner with friends. Sundays at church.

She'd been a do-gooder in college, always trying to spread her message of faith, hope and love. Of course she would spend her Sunday at church. So, the question this morning hadn't been where to find Lauren, but whether or not she was carrying her laptop with her.

She hadn't brought it into the church.

Was it in the car?

Still in the little guesthouse?

In her sister's place?

Maybe she needed to be asked.

Maybe she needed to be forced to hand it over.

What if there were e-mails on it? Hints? Some clue as to what had happened on that gloomy night so long ago?

No. There couldn't be. No one knew. No one who would talk anyway.

Still, there was always the chance that someone else did know. Secrets were hard to keep. Fortunately, blabbing mouths could be silenced. Whatever it took, whatever was necessary. The past would stay where it belonged. Dead and gone. And life would continue as it had for the past ten years. Nothing would keep that from happening.

Nothing and no one.

Including Lauren and her mighty posse of do-gooding friends.

Sounds drifted in from the corridor, heels tapping against the floor, the rustle of fabric. Then silence. Sudden. Unexpected. Filled with every bump-in-the-night imagining, every terrifying nightmare. Lauren stood, straining to hear, waiting for someone to appear in the doorway.

Or some*thing* to appear in the doorway.

Shuffling footsteps. Soft panting breaths. The sound of a stealthy approach. Someone *was* out there. But that was normal. This was a church. It was Sunday. People were supposed to be here.

Trying to move silently?

Working not to be heard?

That didn't sound like a typical way of acting in church.

One way or another, Lauren wasn't going to stand around waiting for the person to appear.

She moved toward the door, jumping back when a pale face peered around the door frame. The woman it belonged to met Lauren's gaze, smiling sheepishly as she stepped into the room, her dark eyes round behind pink-framed glasses, her round face lined with years of laughter.

"Oh, hi. I was wondering who was in here so early. I'm Jenna Case. I teach this class. Do you have a child who's going to attend today?"

The thought of the rather timid-looking Sunday school teacher creeping through the hallway to peek in the room, made Lauren smile. "No, I'm Lauren Owens. I'm a chef and have been working with the Chartrands, trying to create some meal options for Jake."

"Yes. Of course. I've heard your name mentioned several times recently. What can I do for you?"

"I brought some snacks that meet Jake's dietary restrictions. I thought it might be fun for him to share them with the class if that's okay with you."

"Okay? It's a wonderful idea! Maybe you could talk to the class a little while you're at it. Explain the things that Jake is allergic to and how that affects what he can eat."

"Well—"

"He is who God made him and the differences only make him special. I've tried to convey that we're all different in our own way, but there still seems to be curiosity about Jake's allergies. You could really open the lines of communication today." Jenna continued as if she hadn't heard Lauren begin to protest.

"I'm not sure—"

"It'll be fantastic. The kids will have a deeper understanding of their classmate, and I know that would just mean the world to Jake."

It would, of course. Jake was the kind of kid Lauren had been, so eager to fit in, so desperate to belong, but too shy to take the first step toward friendship. "I'd be happy to do that, Ms. Case."

"Great! This is so exciting. A renowned chef here, talking to my students. You know, I really should invite the other Sunday school classes. Maybe the fourth and sixth grades." She paused, her exuberance fading. "If that's okay with you."

"Sure." If she were going to do an impromptu lesson on food allergens she might as well do it big.

"The kids will start arriving in a few minutes. I'm going to let the other teachers know what's going on. Would you like me to bring you some coffee or tea? Water?"

"I'm fine. Thanks."

Jenna bustled out of the room, her energy and excitement still vibrating through the room.

Maybe it was contagious, because Lauren was beginning to think she was right. This *would* be fun. Teaching was the best part of her job. Kids. Adults. Teens. Any time Lauren could impart knowledge about healthy, wholesome foods, she was happy.

If she could get through this morning's lesson without seeing Seth she'd be even happier. The thought brought her mood crashing down.

Helping his son was one thing, spending more time with Seth was another. As far as she was concerned, she'd had a lapse in judgment when she'd gone for coffee with him. She didn't plan to repeat the mistake.

No matter how much she might want to.

And she did want to.

That was the sad, horrifying fact of the matter.

As a teenager Seth had attracted Lauren, his popularity, his confidence, his intelligence appealing to her. As an adult, he intrigued her, his familiarity like hot cocoa on a cold day, something to be savored and enjoyed. But it wasn't the things she remembered that made Lauren want to spend more time with him. It was the things that had changed. He'd matured, grown into himself, become even more of what she'd seen the day she'd met him. More caring. More protective. More willing to give of himself. It would be only too easy to fall under his spell.

Again.

Fortunately, Lauren had matured, too, and she had no intention of letting that happen.

SEVENTEEN

He was falling for her again.

Seth admitted the fact to himself as he stood outside Jake's Sunday school class and listened to Lauren explain what it meant to be allergic to gluten. He hadn't expected it, didn't want it, but couldn't deny what he was feeling. Not nostalgia for days gone by or opportunities lost, but attraction to a beautiful, vibrant woman.

The question was—what did he plan to do about it?

He knew what he wanted to do about it. He wanted to pursue Lauren with the same single-minded determination he had pursued her with in high school. Unfortunately, that hadn't worked out well.

"Dad! What are you doing down here?" Jake ran out of the room, a hoard of children with him, swarming through the corridor in a rush of cheerful energy.

"Waiting for you." That sounded a lot better than "standing out in the hallway listening to an old flame enthrall a group of middle school kids."

"Why? We always meet upstairs."

True. "I figured this time I'd do things differently. Plus, I wanted to talk to Lauren."

"Are you going to invite her for lunch?"

"I wasn't planning to."

"Well, I think we should. To thank her for bringing the cookies and brownies and everything."

"I don't think coming over to our house for leftovers of a meal she prepared counts as thanks, and that's what I was planning for lunch."

"You could make something else. Or we could go out to lunch."

"Jake—"

"Please, Dad?" Jake stared up at him, his freckled face set in earnest appeal. He wouldn't be trying so hard if he knew how much Seth wanted to share a meal with Lauren.

"All right. I'll invite her."

"Great!"

"Go hang with your buddies for a few minutes while I talk to her. Meet me in front of the sanctuary in ten, okay?"

Jake nodded and hurried away, disappearing with the rest of the crowd and leaving the hallway empty.

Lauren was speaking to Jenna Case but looked up as Seth entered the room, her eyes widening, a slight frown marring the smooth lines of her forehead.

"I'm just so glad you agreed to do this for us, Lauren. It went so well." Jenna's enthusiasm bubbled out as she moved toward Seth. "You should have been here, Seth. It was fantastic."

"I'm glad it went well."

"Well? Better than well. I'm hoping Lauren will agree to come to my classroom at school. The information she provided is information every child should have."

"Just let me know where and when, Jenna. I'd be happy to do that."

"We could even have an assembly. Maybe get the whole elementary school involved."

"That's fine. You've got my card. Give me a call, and we'll work things out." Lauren's movements were stiff as she grabbed her purse.

Seth wanted to believe that she was annoyed at being talked into something she'd rather not do, but he suspected her tension had less to do with Jenna's enthusiastic request and more to do with his presence. Too bad. He wasn't planning to leave.

"I will. Thanks again. It really was such a wonderful presentation." Jenna continued to gush as she hurried out of the room, and Seth smiled at her enthusiasm.

"It looks like you've got another fan."

"She was excited to have an open discussion about Jake's allergy problems." She smiled, but Seth knew it was forced and that her fingernails were digging crescents into her palm the way they always had when she'd been angry or upset.

"So was I. Jake has always been embarrassed to bring it up with his friends. This has given him a way to get it out in the open without putting him on the spot."

"That's what I was hoping." She spoke quietly, but her eyes were flashing with emotions he couldn't put his finger on. Anger. Irritation. Worry. Maybe all three.

He understood. He was worried, too. And angry with himself for not being able to turn his back on a woman he knew would be happy to never see him again. "It's what you achieved. You made his day again. I know he won't forget it any time soon. Thanks."

"There's no need to thank me. This is the kind of thing I do for clients."

"Really?"

"Sure. When they need me to."

"And Jake is the first one to need you to, right?"

"Yes, but maybe it's the start of a new trend."

"I really do appreciate it, Lola."

"I didn't do it for you."

"No, but anything that makes Jake happy, makes me happy."

"You're a good father."

"It's my priority."

She nodded and started toward the door. "I'd better get going."

He captured her hand before she could walk away, tugging her forward and running a thumb over the gouges in her palm. "You're upset."

"No, I'm just ready to go home."

"Too bad. Jake asked me to invite you to lunch."

"Lunch isn't a good idea." Her eyes were as blue as the sky on a warm summer day, so vivid it almost hurt to look in them.

"No? I've been thinking it might be."

"That's because it's just lunch to you. To me, it's spending time with a man who…" She shook her head, her frown deepening. "I just think it's a bad idea."

"You're scared, aren't you?" He leaned close, speaking so only she could hear, catching a whiff of the perfume she'd said she'd given to Dee. His heart jumped, his gaze drifting to her mouth before he realized what he was doing and met her eyes again.

She swallowed hard, but didn't lower her gaze or look away. "Scared of you? Not by a long shot."

"Not of me. Of yourself. Of what you still feel for me."

"I don't feel anything for you anymore, Seth."

"I don't believe you."

"You don't have to." Her smile was brittle as she tugged her hand from his and moved toward the stairs. "Please tell Jake I'm sorry I couldn't make it for lunch."

He should let her go. He knew it, but instead of doing what he should, he put a hand on her arm, stopping her again, feeling firm muscles beneath silky fabric and remembering all the times they'd walked together, hands linked, arms pressed close together. "The past few years have taught me a lot of things, Lola. One of them is to never let an opportunity slip through my fingers."

"What opportunity, Seth? To find a chef that can help you better meet your son's dietary needs? To renew an old friendship? To play at a relationship again?"

"I'm not playing."

"Then what are you doing?" She smoothed a hand over her hair, frowning into his eyes, her cheeks pink with irritation.

"The truth? I'm trying to figure out if what's still between us is something I should pursue."

"There is *nothing* between us, Seth."

"Keep telling yourself that, Lauren. Maybe by the time you get back to Savannah you'll believe it."

She stiffened. "I really do need to go. Tell Jake we'll get together some other time."

Eleven years ago, Seth would have tried to cajole her into doing what he'd asked. Eleven years ago, she probably would have given in. But they were both different people now. That was the problem and the blessing. "I'll do that. Enjoy the rest of your day."

Lauren hesitated, as if she'd expected him to push harder for what he wanted. Finally, she smiled, her tension draining away. "I will. Thanks."

She hurried up the stairs, and Seth followed, heading to the sanctuary to find his son, determined to put Lauren out of his mind.

For now.

Jake was exactly where he was supposed to be, talking to friends near the entrance to the sanctuary. He looked up as Seth approached, said something to the lanky kid next to him and ran over. "Is she coming?"

"I'm afraid not."

"Why not?"

"Because she's got a life, kid. She can't spend all her time with you."

"I know. I was just hoping she'd come. Just the two of us is boring sometimes."

"Boring? Me? You've got the wrong guy." Seth ruffled his son's hair and urged him outside.

The sun was high, the day warm and redolent with late-summer foliage. A beautiful day. Not one to be wasted inside. "Tell you what. Why don't we pack up some food and some fishing gear and go to the pond? We can have a picnic, then take the canoe out and see if we can catch dinner."

"Fishing and a picnic? Cool. Do you think Lauren will want to come?"

"No, I do not think she wants to come fishing."

"Maybe you should call and ask."

"Maybe you should be happy to be going with your father."

"How about—"

"Listen, Jake, Lauren doesn't like to fish. There's no way she's going to want to come."

"She might. Some girls do like to fish, you know."

"Not Lauren. And before you ask, I know she doesn't like to fish because we used to be friends."

"You and Lauren?"

"Yep."

"Cool. Did you know her when you were my age?"

"I met her when I was in high school."

"So how come you're not friends anymore?"

"We just lost touch." He opened the car door, letting his son climb in.

"But now that you're in touch you can be friends, right? Like maybe even after she goes back to Savannah, Lauren might come visit sometimes."

Obviously, Jake had a serious crush. Seth wasn't sure whether he should be amused or worried. "How about we talk about something else for a while, buddy?"

"Sure."

"Great." Seth strode around the side of the car, climbed into the driver's seat. "So, let's go have some fun."

An hour later, they'd changed clothes, packed the food, grabbed the fishing gear and were wrangling the canoe onto the top of the car.

Seth's cell phone rang as he tightened the final rope, and he glanced at the number, his pulse leaping as he saw Lauren's name.

"Hello?"

"Seth, it's Lauren. Sorry to interrupt your afternoon, but I think your sister just posted an entry to the Web site's guest book. The last name is different, but the graduation year matches what you told me."

He didn't know what he'd expected her to say, but that wasn't it. "When will it be up for public viewing?"

"I'm posting it now."

"I appreciate you letting me know."

"It's no problem. I know how worried you've been."

"And I'll keep being worried until I actually contact her."

"You should be able to do that. She left an e-mail address."

"Great. I'm going to get going on that now." He started toward the house.

"Will you let me know what happens?" Lauren's question took him by surprise. It shouldn't have. She'd always been compassionate and concerned, quick to offer help and a listening ear. After a few years of dating her, he'd begun to see that as a weakness. Only later, after he'd married a woman who often put herself before others, had he realized just what a gift it was.

"Sure, it'll be a few hours, though. I'm supposed to take Jake fishing."

"That sounds like about as much fun as having a root canal."

"I told Jake you'd say something like that."

"He wanted to invite me?"

"Practically begged me to."

"That's sweet."

"That's a preadolescent crush."

She laughed, the sound seeping through the phone and warming the cold knot of dread that filled him every time he thought about Ellen. "Maybe I should come, then. Show him just how much of a wimp I am when it comes to scaly, slimy things. That might turn his attention in other directions."

"Maybe you should." He let the words hang in the air, waiting for what seemed an eternity before Lauren responded.

"We both know I shouldn't."

"We both know you want to."

"Maybe."

"So come. Jake and I would love to have you."

"All right. I'll come, but I'm not baiting the lines."

"Of course not."

"Or taking the fish off the hooks."

"Jake and I will handle that, too."

"But if you catch something, I may be willing to cook it."

"In that case, we'll have to work extra hard to catch something."

"I'll meet you at your place in twenty minutes."

"Sounds good." He hung up the phone, and turned to his son. "Guess what?"

"What?"

"Lauren's coming fishing after all. Let's go inside and eat while we wait for her."

"Okay." Jake jumped out of the car and hurried toward the house, apparently willing to give up the picnic if that meant having Lauren with them.

Good. Lunch would keep Jake busy while Seth pulled up the Web site and read the guest book entry. Ellen with a different last name Lauren had said. A different Ellen? Or had his sister married? They were questions Seth needed answers to. He prayed he'd get them soon.

EIGHTEEN

Lauren rinsed out the large frying pan and put it in the dishwasher, then grabbed a rag and wiped down the counter. Behind her, Seth and Jake were bent over a math book discussing a problem. Very domestic, very comfortable and very much what she should not be a part of.

She was, though, and she had to admit she was enjoying it. What had begun as a way to convince Jake she wasn't nearly as cool as he thought she was, had turned into a fun outing, her squeamishness about fish and worms making the little boy roar with laughter.

He really was a cute kid.

His father wasn't so bad, either.

Actually, Seth was a lot more than not bad. He was charming, easygoing, great with his son. The fact that he looked like Robert Redford in his prime didn't hurt, either.

"All right, buddy, we're done, and you need to go up to get ready for bed." Seth's words interrupted her thoughts, pulling her away from very dangerous territory.

Lauren waited until the young boy left the room, then grabbed her purse, anxious to leave before she started building a fantasy future out of a simple meal of fish and salad. "That was fun, Seth. Thanks for inviting me."

"Thanks for coming." He leaned against the doorjamb, his eyes the color of misty valleys and deep forests; lush, filled with life.

"I'd better go."

"Probably." As he spoke, he moved toward her, his gaze never leaving hers. "But I'm hoping you won't."

"Staying would be a mistake."

"You've been saying that about a lot of things lately, Lola, but this doesn't feel like a mistake." He cupped her neck, his fingers tangling in her hair. "Neither does this."

One tug and she was in his arms. One look and she was drowning, his gaze so intense she shivered. "Seth, I really don't think we should be doing this."

"Then walk away."

She should. She really should. So why was she still standing in his arms? Why was she still staring into his eyes? Why did every part of her being long to lean into his strength? "Whatever you're thinking, it isn't going to happen. I'm not a teenager anymore. I've changed. I don't want the same things I used to."

He bent so that his lips were close to her ear. "You may have changed, Lola, but you feel the same when you're in my arms. Like you belong."

"I don't. Not anymore."

"Stay a while longer and you might change your mind."

"Seth—" The phone rang, the shrill tone cutting through the moment and whatever was between them.

Lauren slid out of Seth's arms. "You'd better get that."

"The answering machine will pick it up."

"It might be important." She stepped away, putting space between them so that she could breathe again.

"So is this." He tugged her toward him again, but stopped when a feminine voice filled the room.

"Seth… It's Ellen. I got your e-mail. I know—"

He picked up the phone, his hand tightening around Lauren's. "I was hoping you'd call me, sis."

"I'm going to go." Lauren mouthed the words, squeezing Seth's hand before heading outside. Ellen was alive and well. It was a good way to end the evening. One less person missing, one less person to worry about. There'd be a good ending for Seth and his sister. Lauren prayed Payton Bell and Josie Skerritt would have the same. Both had been active in Magnolia College's Campus Christian Fellowship club. Lauren couldn't believe they'd leave college and never look back unless something had happened that prevented them from getting in touch.

She shuddered at the thought of what that something might be. Both had been young and healthy. Neither of them had been pregnant. At least, she didn't think they had been. Still, she couldn't get either woman out of her mind as she started back toward Dee's place. Someone's life had been cut short ten years ago. Could it have been one of Lauren's friends?

Her cell phone rang as she pulled into the carriage house driveway, and she answered. "I'm back so you can stop worrying."

"That's not why I'm calling."

She'd expected Dee, and Seth's voice took her by surprise. "Seth. Hi. How'd things go with Ellen?"

"Not good." His voice had a gritty edge as if deep emotion were scratching along his throat.

"What is it? What's going on?"

"Ellen explained why she left ten years ago and hasn't been in contact since. I…didn't like what she had to say."

Whatever it was, it had to be bad. Seth had never gotten upset over little things. Even big things usually didn't throw him off his stride.

"Do you need me to come back?" The offer was out before she could think it through.

"No, I just need to talk."

"About your sister?"

"About my son." His words were clipped, his tone harsh, and Lauren's heart lurched, her stomach clenching with a million possibilities.

"Is something wrong with him?"

"Not if we ignore the fact that he might not be my son."

"What are you talking about? Of course Jake is your son."

"That's not what my wife thought. According to Ellen, Donna was terrified that Jake might not be mine."

"Ellen was never around, Seth. How could she possibly know what your wife was thinking?"

"She came to visit several months after Jake was born to stay with Donna while I was away on business. Jake had been really sick, and I thought it would help Donna to have someone around."

"And your wife told her she was afraid Jake wasn't yours? Were they such good friends?"

"No, they barely knew each other. According to Ellen, she woke up around five one morning, went to the kitchen for coffee and overheard Donna on the phone with an ex-boyfriend."

"Someone you knew?"

"A guy she'd been seeing before we met. As far as I

knew, they hadn't been in contact for years, but I guess I was wrong. Apparently, my wife had met up with him again after our wedding. When she learned that Jake's health problems were due to food allergies, she was sure they had a hereditary cause. I don't have food allergies. Neither did Donna."

"That doesn't mean Jake isn't yours. Allergies aren't always hereditary."

"Yeah, I know, but apparently Donna didn't. Maybe she was uninformed or maybe a guilty conscience got the best of her. Ellen heard her say that the timing was bad and that she wasn't sure if Jake was mine, that if this guy had food allergies in his family, she wanted to know about it so she could make a decision about what to do." His words were harsh and angry, and Lauren's stomach knotted even tighter.

"I'm sorry, Seth."

"Me, too. Donna and I didn't always see eye to eye, but I thought we were making the best of our marriage, creating a good life for our son. I guess I was kidding myself."

"None of us wants to think the worst of someone we love."

"Love is a choice we make. I'd chosen to love Donna. I thought she'd done the same with me. Obviously, I was wrong."

"Maybe Ellen is wrong about what she heard. Maybe she misunderstood."

"There's no chance of that. Ellen confronted Donna, and Donna was distraught enough to admit the truth. She had an affair. Jake might have been the result. When Ellen said she was going to call and tell me to come home, Donna ran. Five minutes later she lost control of her car and slammed into a tree."

"That was the accident that took her life?"

"Yeah. She wasn't wearing a seat belt. I always wondered about that. She'd been such a stickler for it. Now I know why. She was too upset to think clearly."

"I don't understand why Ellen didn't tell you this before."

"I'd lost my wife and was going to be raising Jake on my own. She wasn't sure how I'd take it, so she went to my parents to ask them to help break the news to me. They accused her of trying to cause problems."

"Is there any possibility that they were right?"

"Ellen was a lot of things, but she was never a liar. She says she stayed away for ten years because my parents forbade her from telling me the truth. She didn't want to cause more strife in the family, so she left. Now she's got a husband, a family, and she wants to be part of my life again. I believe her. I'd better go. I need to think this through some more. Decide what I'm going to do about it." The line went dead, the silence in Lauren's car so thick, so filled with sorrow, she thought she'd choke on it.

What would it be like to find out that a child you loved, that you'd raised, might not be yours?

She couldn't even imagine it.

She thought of the young boy—his freckled cheeks, his strawberry blond hair, his forest-green eyes. He was a younger version of Seth. Even his lanky arms and legs reminded her of Seth when he'd been younger. It was inconceivable that a child who looked so much like his father wasn't related by blood.

Blood. Seth had a rare blood type. AB negative.

If Jake had the same blood type, the same hair color, the

same eyes, it would be almost ludicrous to believe he wasn't Seth's son.

If.

Lauren lifted her cell phone. Dropped it again.

She could call.

Or she could go back.

But going back would say something about her relationship with Seth, something she didn't want to admit but couldn't deny. Seth had been right when he said it felt as if she belonged in his arms, but there was so much more to it than that. After eleven years apart, eleven years of not speaking to or seeing each other, they still fit into each other's lives. Easily. As if they'd never been apart. As if they belonged together.

Ridiculous.

She shook her head, her hands clenched on the steering wheel. Ridiculous or not, it was the truth.

She was going to get hurt again.

She knew it.

But somehow that didn't matter nearly as much as being there for Seth tonight. He needed a friend. She could be that. Whether or not she could be something more remained to be seen.

Too much hurt.

Too many broken promises.

A world of experiences that hadn't been shared.

God's plan. Working out His way. In His time.

If only she knew what that was. If only she knew why her life had intersected with Seth's again, but she didn't, so she'd just have to trust that in the end it would all work out the way God intended.

She sighed and backed the car out of the driveway. For tonight, she wouldn't be analytic and cautious. For tonight she'd just do what she thought was right.

People never did what was expected of them. That was the biggest problem in the world. Too many people more concerned about themselves than others. Too many people whose only thoughts were for their own wants and needs.

A few less people like that wouldn't be a bad thing. That wasn't in the plan, of course, but sometimes plans had to change. Sometimes new ones needed to be made.

Like now.

Three hours waiting for Lauren to return, five minutes of breathless anticipation, and then…nothing. She hadn't even gotten out of the car. Time to stop waiting.

Lauren would just have to miss the show. Such a shame. But time was ticking by and eventually Dee would be back home. It was now or never, and never was not an option.

Clouds covered the moon and draped the night in blackness, the shadows a friend to the creatures that crept through the darkness. Raccoons, opossums, reptiles, rodents. People with secrets to hide.

So many secrets.

So many failures.

Here's to success.

A quick, hard throw, shattering glass, the alarm sounding shrill and insistent.

Maybe Lauren would get the hint this time.

She'd better.

NINETEEN

Seth barely heard the soft tap at the door, and at first thought it was nothing more than the throbbing pulse of his heart; Donna's betrayal echoing through his head again and again. When he finally realized someone was at the door, he stood, not sure he wanted to answer it. He'd been through a lot in his life, but tonight's revelations were the worst so far.

The knock sounded again, this time a little louder and a little more insistent.

He'd spent the past few days researching the deaths that had occurred during the years preceding Lauren's graduation. He'd tried to pinpoint any commonalities in the victims, but in the end had come up blank. He'd been prepared to keep searching.

He hadn't been prepared to hear that his son might not be biologically his.

The person at the door knocked again, this time three quick taps followed by two slower ones.

Lola?

That had been their knock when they'd been young and romantic enough to have secret signals. It had been years since he'd thought about that, years since he'd wanted to.

He pulled open the door, looked into concerned blue eyes, his heart constricting, his breath freezing in his lungs. "I didn't expect to see you again tonight."

"I thought maybe you needed a friend."

"I do." He tugged her into the house and pulled her into his arms, his face pressed into soft curls. She smelled of flowers and sunshine, vanilla and cinnamon, comfort and home.

"Are you okay?" Her hands curved around his waist, her fingers firm and warm through his cotton shirt.

"I have to be."

"I know you have to pretend to be, but are you really?" She leaned back, her hand pressing against his cheek, the sadness in her eyes as raw and sharp as his felt.

"No. Jake is my son. It's killing me to think someone else is his father, that someone else may have parental rights. If that's true, I may lose him."

"Don't say that, Seth. There's no way someone is going to take him away from you."

"No? There are plenty of legal cases that prove otherwise. The fact that I've raised him since he was born won't be weighted evenly against biology." That was the real heartbreak. Donna's betrayal was a blow, but the thought of losing Jake, of sending his shy, timid son to live with someone he didn't know was breaking Seth's heart.

"You're assuming that Jake isn't your biological child."

"No, I'm just concerned about what will happen if he's not."

"He looks just like you, Seth. The same hair, the same eyes."

"There are plenty of kids out there with red hair and

green eyes who aren't mine, and plenty of kids that don't look anything like their biological parents."

"I know, but he really does remind me of you."

"I don't think that'll hold much water in a court of law." He tried to smile, but failed miserably. One phone call, one discussion with a sister he hadn't seen in years and his life had been turned upside down.

"Why would it even get that far? Jake is yours. If your wife's ex was interested in fathering him, he would have come around after she called him."

"Probably, but I have to be sure. If I had another son out in the world somewhere, I'd want to know."

"That's because you're a good guy."

"I don't feel like such a good one right now. Right now, I feel like tearing something apart." Someone, actually. Donna. Gone ten years and still reaping the rewards of a life lived for self rather than others.

The bitter thought about a woman he'd loved, a woman who'd died way too soon, made him feel like the worst kind of heel.

He stepped away from Lauren, his hands trailing along her shoulders and arms before finally releasing their hold. "I appreciate you coming by, Lola, but I'm not the best company right now."

"Who would be? You've been living your life, thinking things were one way and then suddenly you realize that nothing is what you thought."

"You sound like you know all about it."

"I lived it."

"When I broke up with you."

"On a smaller scale, but yes."

"I was an idiot."

"You were assertive, driven, wanting adventure. I was quiet, content and ready to settle. We weren't meant to work out."

"Not then."

Her cheeks heated, and she shifted, her gaze dropping. "I was thinking about you and Jake. You've got AB negative blood, right?"

"Yes."

"Does Jake?"

"You know, I'm not sure. Besides his allergies, we haven't had any major health concerns. I'm sure his blood was typed when he was born, though."

"Can you find out, because if he does, that would be pretty clear proof that he's your biological child."

"Proof, but not definitive. AB negative is rare, but Jake having it doesn't mean anything unless Donna's ex has a different blood type."

"So, you just need to find out and you'll have the proof."

"Easier said than done. I never met the guy, never knew his name, and Donna's not around to ask."

"Someone will know. Her friends or family."

"Maybe. It's been a long time, but I'll start asking around." Even though he'd rather not. It would be so much easier to forgot what Ellen had told him, to ignore what he knew was his obligation.

"What about Jake?"

"He doesn't need to know any of this unless I find out he's not biologically mine."

"Is there anything I can do to help?"

"Just having you here has helped."

"I'm glad. We all need a friend sometimes." She brushed a loose curl from her cheek and smiled. "I know everything is going to be okay, Seth. God won't let you lose your son."

"I hope you're right. When I was younger, I couldn't imagine myself living the kind of life I do now. A house in a small town, PTA dad, working as an estate lawyer. Now I can't imagine living any other way."

"It'll be okay." She squeezed his hand, and he captured hers before she could pull it away. Lauren had been the first woman to capture his heart. If he hadn't been such a fool, she might have been the only one. Staring into her eyes was like looking at the past and the future.

"I meant what I said about us. Just because we didn't work out years ago, doesn't mean we can't work out now."

"If that's what we want, but it's not. At least it's not what I want." Her gaze was direct, her eyes silvery blue and unreadable.

"Isn't it?" Because he was pretty sure it was what he wanted.

"Truthfully? I don't know. I just know I don't want to be hurt again." She shrugged, her shoulders thin beneath a gray cardigan, her skin the silky smoothness of rose petals. He wanted to reach out, run a finger along the curve of her cheek, feel the softness of her skin, press his lips to the tender flesh behind her ear, follow the angle of her jaw to her lips.

A mistake? Maybe, but right now he didn't care.

"I was young and stupid. I'm older now and hopefully wiser. I won't hurt you again." He moved close, cupping her jaw, tasting the warmth of her lips, a gentle kiss that sent heat spearing through him.

She sucked in a breath, stared into his eyes. "I'm older,

too, and definitely wiser." She stepped from his arms. "I'm not looking for a relationship, Seth. Not with you. Not with anybody."

"Sometimes the thing we're not looking for is what we end up getting."

"Maybe you're right. Only time will tell, I guess. Speaking of which…" She glanced at her watch and frowned. "It's late. I'd better be getting back."

"Afraid you'll turn into a pumpkin if you're not home before midnight?" He allowed the conversation to shift, allowed her to have the space she wanted, but the ache in his chest settled more firmly as she stepped outside. At least with her here he had something to focus on besides his conversation with Ellen and all that it had revealed.

"Actually, I'm afraid if I'm not home by midnight Dee will send out a posse to round me up."

"I can see her doing that. She's always been very protective of you."

"Yeah, well she's been worse lately. I think between the vandalism and the phone call, she got spooked."

"She's not the only one. No more problems since then, though, right?"

"None. Life has gone right back to normal and predictable."

"You make it sound like that's a bad thing."

"It's not. It's just what it is." She smiled again, but there were questions in her eyes and a sadness he knew was only partially to do with Ellen's news about Jake. "I'd really better go. Call me if you need my help with anything."

"Same for you."

She'd already started toward her car, but she turned

back toward him, darkness hiding her expression. "A week ago, I was dreading seeing you. I hoped you wouldn't show up at the fund-raiser dinner."

"I kind of got that."

"Now I'm glad you were there, glad we're getting to know each other again. You've turned into a good man, a devoted father. Nothing can take that away. Good night." She got in her car and drove away, the sound of the engine fading and leaving Seth standing in silence.

He hadn't expected Lauren to come, but he was glad she had. Discussing Ellen's claims had eased some of his tension. She'd been right. Jake was Seth's spitting image. Everyone said so. If he had the same blood type, Seth could put the whole thing to bed, confident that Jake was not just his son, but also his biological child.

That was all he wanted right now.

That and another chance at having what he'd once turned his back on. He could only pray he'd get both.

He raked a hand through his hair, inhaling crisp evening air and the scent of freshly cut grass, staring into the night, wondering what tomorrow would bring.

He spoke softly. "Lord, You know what the future is going to bring. Give me peace about everything that is happening and help me to find the answers I need about Jake quickly."

Because he needed the truth.

The sooner the better.

He wanted to go inside the house and phone Jake's pediatrician, but the office would be closed. Waiting wasn't something he did well. He preferred to take charge, move forward, get started. This time he couldn't. There was no plan for this. No way to make it easier.

Time. That's what it would take. Patience, determination. Eventually he'd get the answers he sought. Until then, he'd just have to be patient and trust that God was in control, because he sure knew he wasn't. That kiss had proved it. Lauren's lips, soft and warm beneath his. That was going to stay with him for a while.

He sighed and went back inside, closing the door on the night and wishing he could close the door on his troubles just as easily.

TWENTY

He'd kissed her.

And she'd been happy about it.

Lauren wasn't sure which was more appalling.

She'd dated other men since Seth, kissed other men, even imagined a future with them. None had fit. None had made her feel as if she belonged. In the end, that had been enough to send her running and to convince her that life alone might not be such a bad thing.

She needed to remember that.

And remember how many promises Seth had made and then broken.

Years ago. He's changed. You know he has.

She did, but she wasn't sure that was enough, because Seth wasn't the only one who'd changed. She had, too, but not as much as he probably thought. She'd made a life and career for herself, carved a reputation as a premier Savannah chef and had imagined giving that up a million times. Imagined living the life she'd always wanted with a husband, kids, a charming old house with a white picket fence and vegetable garden. The beauty of that dream hadn't faded over time. She just wasn't sure she could have it with Seth. As much as she saw the changes in him, he must be looking at the changes in her, thinking she was a world traveler, a woman with excitement and adventure flowing through her blood.

She was far from that.

Once he realized it, he'd be as bored with her and their relationship as he had been years ago. That was something she didn't want to experience again.

So, no more staring into deep green eyes. No more standing in the kitchen while Seth and his son bent over homework.

No more kisses.

She sighed, turning onto Dee's street, her heart lodging in her throat as she caught sight of a police car sitting in her sister's driveway.

She pulled up in front of the house, jumped from the car, racing to Dee's front door and banging on the wood.

Seconds later, the door flew open.

"Lauren! Where have you been? I've been worried sick."

"I told you I was going over to Seth's for a while."

"A while? It's nearly midnight." Dee's eyes were red and puffy, her face pale, tracks of tears running through her makeup. "Mr. Robinson next door said he saw you come back over an hour ago."

"I did, but something came up, and I went back out."

"Something that prevented you from answering your cell phone? I've been calling you for forty minutes."

"I left it in my car. What's going on?"

"What's going on is that I thought you'd been kidnapped or worse! I was imagining never seeing you again. I was getting ready to call Mom and Dad and tell them the worst had happened."

"Why? What are the police doing here?"

"The carriage house has been vandalized again. A brick was thrown through a window, and there's blood all over the front door."

"Blood?"

"Blood. The alarm company called me to report a break-in. When I got here, the police were already checking things out. They think it's animal blood. I don't care what kind of blood it is, it's creepy. Come inside," She pulled Lauren into the house. "Standing out here is giving me the willies."

She wasn't the only one.

Lauren shivered as she stepped into Dee's kitchen.

Blood on the door of the carriage house. A brick thrown through the window. The crank call. Obviously someone had an issue with Lauren being in town. Who and why was something she couldn't even begin to imagine.

"Want some coffee?" Dee poured her a cup before she even responded, setting it down on the table, her hand shaking. "I've got to tell you, I've never been so worried in my life. When you didn't answer your phone I was absolutely sure something unimaginable had happened to you. I never want to feel that way again." She shook her head.

"I'm sorry. I had no idea any of this was happening."

"How could you know some idiot was going to decide to smash a window and vandalize the place? And save your apologies for the girls. I called all of them to ask if they'd seen you. They'll be here any minute."

Lauren sighed, grabbing the coffee and taking a sip. "I suppose it was time for another get-together."

"Yeah, but not at midnight. I'm going to call and let them know you're fine."

A sharp knock sounded at the door, and Lauren smiled. "I think it's too late."

Five minutes later, Cassie, Jennifer and Steff were all sipping coffee and staring out the back window, watching as the police continued searching for evidence. Lauren was still shaky, but her friends' presences made the situation seem a lot less frightening than it was.

"It looks like they're dusting for prints. Do you think they'll find anything?" Jennifer leaned closer to the window, her black hair spilling down her back, loose and a little tangled as if she'd jumped out of bed and run from the house without bothering to brush it.

"I hope so. They need to find the sicko and put him in jail where he belongs." Dee's vehement reply couldn't hide the fear in her eyes.

Lauren dropped an arm around her shoulder, wishing she believed that the police would find the person responsible, but she was starting to doubt there'd be a quick solution to her troubles. "Whoever it is must have known we weren't going to be home tonight."

"Maybe. Or maybe he was hoping we'd be home and was disappointed that we weren't here to experience the full impact of his actions."

"You're assuming it's a man." Steff turned away from the window, her eyes shadowed with fatigue. "Women do stuff like this, too."

"True, but this feels like a guy thing to me. First trashing the guesthouse, then the crank call, then the brick and the blood." Dee shrugged.

"You forgot the guest book entry Lauren received." Cassie took a seat at the table. Of the four, Lauren thought she was the only one who didn't look tired, but, then, in all the time they'd known each other, Lauren had never known her to be down or tired.

"Do you really think that has something to do with the vandalism and phone threat? It seems to me, they're completely different things." Jennifer took a sip of coffee and sat next to Cassie.

"I think we're about to find out. It looks like the cops are done. One of them is heading this way."

"Detective Anderson." Dee hurried to open the back door. "Hopefully he can tell us exactly what's going on."

A pipe dream, but Lauren didn't say that to Dee. Let her think there might be an end to this in sight. Lauren's own thoughts were a little more grim.

"Ladies." Detective Anderson stepped into the kitchen, nodding his head in greeting, his hard expression doing little to allay Lauren's fears.

"Did you find anything?" Dee's tight question reflected the tension in the room.

"A note." He held up an evidence bag, spearing Lauren with an intense stare. "I'm hoping you can shed some light on it."

"I can try." What was it? A note from an angry client? An ex-boyfriend? A deranged stalker? She didn't think she had any of those in her life, but maybe there was something she hadn't thought of, someone who was desperate to show her just how angry he was. Was the note a death threat? A blow-by-blow description of what the vandal planned to do if he got his hands on her? Every thriller she'd ever watched, every suspense novel she'd ever read beat at the back of her mind, her heart pounding with anxiety.

"It says, 'Stop sticking your nose into other people's business.' Do you have any idea what it refers to?"

That was it? The big threat? Lauren almost laughed with relief. Only the situation wasn't funny. Maybe a little less grim than she'd imagined, but not funny. "I don't know. I'm doing the same things I've always done. Cooking, meeting with friends. I can't see how any of that would bother anyone."

"You're also doing the Magnolia College: Where Are They Now Web site." He pulled out a notepad, jotted something on it.

"Yes, but I don't think that's the same as sticking my nose into someone's business."

"You'd be surprised, ma'am. People with guilty consciences often see threats where there are none. Some things have come to light recently that might be making someone very nervous."

"You're talking about the woman whose remains were found at the college." Steff drummed her fingers against the tabletop, nervous energy coming off her in waves.

"Our forensic expert hasn't determined the cause of death, but people who die of natural causes don't normally wind up buried beneath a sidewalk." He shrugged. "And we're dealing with a woman between the ages of eighteen and twenty-four. Not an elderly woman who might have stumbled and gotten trapped, or a young kid who might have been playing around."

"You think she was murdered." Cassie sounded as appalled as Lauren felt every time she contemplated such a violent end to the woman's life.

"What I think doesn't matter. A drug overdose, an accident, foul play—until the forensics specialist finishes with his examination of the remains we won't know. What we do know is that something happened at the college ten years ago. Now, you're running a Web site that's designed to bring alumni together, and someone is warning you to stay out of other people's business. It's a stretch to think it's all a coincidence."

"There has to be a way to find out who's doing this. What about the phone call Lauren received? Were you able to trace the call?" Steff stood, paced the room, her edginess making Lauren feel antsy.

"A pay phone in town. Too many prints on it to try and get a match, but we'll find the guy. Trust me on that. Magnolia Falls isn't a big place. Magnolia College isn't a big school. People know each other. They know each other's business. It's only a matter of time before someone comes forward with information that will lead us to our perp."

"How much time, Detective? Because it seems to me the incidents are escalating, and I'm worried for my sister."

"I wish I could tell you that, ma'am. We're doing all we can. My suggestion to all of you would be to close down the Web site and let whatever trouble you're stirring up settle down again."

Lauren didn't like the implication behind the words. That somehow she'd brought on her own problems. "I don't think we're stirring up trouble so much as helping people find each other again."

"Hey, I'm not knocking the Web site or what you're doing. It's a great way to get in touch with old friends. But if, as I suspect, the Web site's launch somehow precipitated the crimes against you, it might be best to close it down. At least until we find the person that's committing these crimes."

"Understood." But Lauren didn't like the idea of letting someone scare her into giving up on the Web site. Contacting old friends, making sure they were safe, that was the goal, and she didn't want to let it go. She'd discuss it with the others, but as of now, she had no intention of backing off and giving in.

"Is there anything else that's changed in your life recently? A broken relationship? A new one?"

There was Seth, but Lauren wasn't sure that counted as a relationship.

No? Then what was the kiss about?

The thought flitted through her mind, but she ignored it. "Not that I can think of."

"All right. We'll keep looking then. I've already talked to the neighbors. They didn't see anything, but that doesn't mean no one else did. We'll ask around, see what happens. With no evidence, it's hard, but eventually something will break and we'll have our guy."

"You said you weren't able to find any evidence, but what about the blood?" Jennifer almost seemed to shudder as she asked the question.

"We took samples of it. It's probably animal blood. We'll know for sure soon."

"That's sickening." Cassie wrinkled her nose, her bright eyes dark and filled with disgust, worry and fear. All the things Lauren was feeling. All the things she was sure the other women were feeling, as well.

"I wish I could say it's the worst I've ever seen, but the world is filled with sick people." Detective Anderson tucked the notepad back into his pocket. "I'll call once we have the test results. In the meantime, you might want to stay here instead of in the guesthouse, Ms. Owens."

"All right."

"And if anything else happens, or if you think of something that might be relevant to what's been going on, give me a call. No matter how insignificant it seems."

"I will. Thanks for your help, Detective."

"No problem. Just be careful, ma'am. Things like this can escalate quickly. If our perp isn't someone playing games and trying to scare you, we may be dealing with a person who doesn't have a moral compass. Someone who thinks it's fine to do whatever it takes to keep his secrets hidden."

Lauren's heart thumped at his words, her stomach clenching. "Meaning?"

"Meaning anything could happen." He strode out the front door, got into his car, offering a quick wave before driving away.

"That went well." Dee's sarcasm split the silence, and Lauren turned to face her sister.

"It went as well as it could. There's not much Detective Anderson can do if there's no evidence."

"I know he's doing the best he can. I'm just worried and that's making me angry."

"Don't be, Dee." Cassie put a hand on her arm. "This is scary, but God is in control of it. Everything is going to work out okay."

"That's easy to say. It's not so easy to believe." Dee's words were a jab in Lauren's heart. Years ago, Dee had attended church faithfully. At some point she'd turned her back on it and her faith. Lauren couldn't pinpoint when the change had taken place and didn't know why. She only knew it had happened.

"It's not so hard to believe. God has gotten me through plenty of things, Dee. I'm going to have to trust that He'll get me through this."

"None of those things involved threatening messages and blood."

"No, but I'll still be okay."

"Of course you will." Jennifer spoke quickly, perhaps hoping to forestall any further discussion that might upset Dee. "We'll just shut down the Web site for a while, and everything will get back to normal."

Lauren didn't think it was going to be that easy. "I don't think that's going to solve the problem."

"I agree, and not just because the Web site is boosting alumni involvement." Steff ran a hand over her hair and frowned. "The way I see it, if what's happening has something to do with the body that was found, it's not going to stop because we shut down the Web site."

"That's exactly what I'm thinking. How about you, Cassie?" If they were going to decide on whether or not to shut down the Web site, everyone needed to have a say.

"I hate to say it, but I think you and Steff are right. I can't see that shutting down the Web site at this point will do any good. If we've opened a can of worms, closing it up again isn't going to put them back in."

"Nice image, Cassie, but maybe you're right. Maybe we shouldn't shut down the Web site. Of course, if we're voting we'll need to let Kate in on it." Jennifer smiled and the tension in the room eased. "She'll be upset if we don't include her. As a matter of fact, she's probably waiting by her phone, praying that Lauren is okay."

"You're right, I'd better call her." Dee reached for the

phone, but it rang before she could pick it up. "I bet that's her now."

She lifted it. "Hey, I was just going to call you." She listened, smiled, her gaze on Lauren. "Sorry about that. I thought you were someone else. Lauren is right here."

She held out the phone, mouthing Seth's name in an exaggerated way that had everyone staring at Lauren.

"Hey, what's up?" Her cheeks were warm. She told herself it was because her closest friends were staring at her as if she'd lost her mind.

"I heard there was trouble at your sister's house again. I wanted to make sure you were okay."

"Heard there was trouble? From whom?"

"Your sister's neighbor, Jim Robinson, is one of my clients. He knows we're friends. I guess he thought I might want to know."

"Did you?"

"You know I did."

Lauren's cheeks heated even more, and she glared at her sister and friends, hoping they'd give her some privacy. When none of them took the hint, she walked into Dee's office and closed the door. "Thanks for your concern, but I really am okay."

"What happened?"

"Someone threw a brick through the carriage house window." She hesitated.

"What else?"

"Blood on the front door and a note for me that said I should keep my nose out of other people's lives."

"I don't like this, Lola. Too many things are happening, and you're right in the middle of them."

"Not by choice."

"No, but if you go back to Savannah you might be safer. Why don't you head home tomorrow?"

"Because I've still got a week of my vacation left, and I'm not going to let anyone keep me from having it."

"Are you sure that's the best idea?"

"No, but I'm not sure it's the worst, either." She leaned her hip against the corner of Dee's desk, the cadence of Seth's voice bringing back memories of other phone conversations. Of whispered words in the middle of the night. Of quiet laughter while the rest of the house slept. In the months after Seth went off to his first year of college, Lauren had called him at all times of the day and night. When she'd been lonely, scared, worried, he'd been there. For a while.

"If it keeps you in harm's way, it is the worst idea. Think about it, Lola. Things were fine until you came back to Magnolia Falls."

"And leaving the area doesn't guarantee I'll be safe again. Besides, I'm not sure I'm in any physical danger now. Someone is upset with me, but that doesn't mean they plan to harm me."

"Blood on a door seems pretty violent to me." Seth's words were grim, and she imagined him pacing across his living room, his chin shadowed with stubble, his thick hair spiked from running his fingers through it.

"I know, but at least here, I'm with Dee. At home, I'll be by myself."

"Just be careful, Lola. I don't want anything to happen to you." His tone was warm and intimate, as if he were sharing a secret meant only for her, and she felt herself melting into it, responding as she had so often when they'd dated, her mind spiraling back to a time when she'd believed every word he'd told her.

"I was thinking about you today." His words filled her with longing and a fierce need to graduate high school and follow him to Magnolia College.

"What were you thinking?"

"That you're the most beautiful girl I've ever known and that I can't wait to see you this weekend."

Her cheeks heated at his words, and she tugged at the end of her ponytail. She'd been so afraid that he'd forget her once he left Savannah, so afraid that he'd find someone else. *"I missed you, too. I can't wait to see you, either."*

"Lola, you always tell me what I want to hear."

She laughed, the sound pealing out into the darkness of her bedroom, filling the room with the pure joy talking to Seth always brought.

"Lola? Are you still there?" He spoke quietly, and she forced back the tears that were clogging her throat.

"Where else would I be?"

"Running from me?"

"Not this time, but I am going to have to go."

"Then I'll let you. Take care, Lola."

"You, too." She hung up before she was tempted to let the conversation linger for a while longer.

Seth. Still too much a part of her thoughts and feelings, too big a force in her life. Years ago, she'd learned to live without him. Did she really want to go back to those days of needy affection?

No way.

Did she want to go back to Seth?

That was a much harder question to answer.

She stepped back out into the hall, hoping her confusion wasn't apparent on her face. Long explanations weren't something she wanted to give. Especially because she wasn't sure what they would be.

Four pairs of eyes looked into hers, four faces displayed emotions ranging from amusement to anxiety. "What?"

"*What?* What do you mean, *what?*" Cassie grabbed her arm, nearly jumping with excitement. "Seth Chartrand called you at half past midnight, and you think you can just saunter out here and act like nothing happened? I don't think so, girlfriend."

"Too bad, because nothing did happen. Seth wanted to make sure Dee and I were okay."

"Really? How sweet. Did he even bother to mention my name." Dee grinned, her blue eyes flashing with amusement.

"Not quite, but he came close."

Dee laughed and the others joined in.

And for a moment Lauren allowed herself to forget the danger that seemed to be dogging her, the strangeness of her renewed relationship with Seth, her own worries and fears. Surrounded by good friends, she could relax, elusive safety within reach. Eventually, Jennifer, Steff and Cassie would leave, Dee would head off to bed and Lauren would be alone. For now, though, they were here, and Lauren had to be content with that.

TWENTY-ONE

Lauren woke late, groggy from restless sleep, her mind fuzzy. Her dreams had been filled with half-formed images and shadowy monsters, faces of people she'd once known. Payton Bell. Josie Skerritt. Seth.

Even in her sleep, he'd been on her mind.

He'd kissed her. The memory of it had lingered long into the night.

A quick shower didn't revive her, and she dragged herself to the kitchen for coffee, smiling as she read the note Dee had left for her. Ever organized, she'd already managed to contract a cleaning company to wash the blood off the carriage house door and had hired a local contractor to fix the window. She also told Lauren to call Seth and let him know she'd survived the night.

That part of the letter was one Lauren planned to ignore. She'd admit that she was tempted not to. Calling Seth seemed like such a natural thing to do.

Scratch that.

It was not comfortable or natural. It was a habit. Or at least an old habit revisited.

Maybe working would get her mind off Seth. Returning from vacation next week would be hectic if she didn't start planning now. She went outside to grab her laptop and cell phone from the car, knowing that nothing could keep her mind from circling back to the one place it shouldn't be, but determined to give it her best shot.

Gray clouds hung low from a steely sky, the scent of moisture heavy in the air. Usually, she loved this kind of day, the gloomy rain making her want to settle into a chair with coffee, a plate of cookies and a recipe book. Last night had skewed her perspective, though, and instead of standing in the cool, damp air, she glanced around, her heart beating too fast, her mouth dry. The darkness of the day seemed sinister, the hulking trees that lined Dee's property the perfect hiding place.

Of course there was no one there. As she'd told Seth, she really didn't think she was in danger. That didn't stop her from yanking her laptop and cell phone from the car and running back into the house. She was out of breath when she slammed the door and bolted it, fear racing along her spine and warning her that anything could happen. That some poor woman had died alone ten years ago, and there was nothing but an alarm system and a door lock to keep it from happening to her right now.

Craziness.

No one was after her. No one wanted her dead.

She'd better keep that in mind, or she'd never walk outside again.

Her cell phone rang and she jumped, her heart slamming in her chest. Another crank call? Another warning?

She glanced at the number, saw Seth's name and

answered, ignoring the way her pulse jumped and her blood warmed. "Hello?"

"Hello? Um, this is Jake Chartrand. Um—"

"Jake, what's up? Is everything okay?" Had he heard her talking to his father the previous night? Had something happened to Seth?

"Yeah, but I had an allergic reaction to something I ate this morning. I got all swollen up and blotchy, and we had to use the EpiPen. The doctor said I'm fine, but Dad said I had to stay home anyway."

"That makes sense. Are you feeling better?"

"I'm still blotchy, but I'm not swollen."

"Glad to hear it. So, did you call me for a reason?"

"Yes. You see…well, our class is having a party Wednesday, and I wanted to bring cookies that I can eat and maybe cupcakes, too."

Relief coursed through her, and she set her laptop on the kitchen table, leaned a shoulder against the wall, smiling as she pictured Jake's freckled face. "I see. Does your father know you're calling?"

"Not really."

"Not really?"

"He doesn't. I didn't ask."

"Because you knew he'd say no?"

"Kind of."

"You know that wasn't the right thing to do, Jake. Where did you get my number?"

"Dad has a card with your phone number on it by the phone. I'm sorry I called without permission. It's just Dad is at a meeting, and Reese is at school. Mrs. Williams is babysitting. I figured since I couldn't get in touch with Dad maybe it would be okay."

"I think you know it wasn't."

"I do now."

Lauren chuckled, imagining Jake's face going three shades of red. "I have a feeling you did before, too."

"The thing is, Sunday was so much fun, and I started thinking how we were going to be having a party Wednesday because it's Allie Sanders's last day at school. She's moving to Texas. We're going to have a goodbye party the last fifteen minutes of class."

"Sounds like fun."

"Yeah. Except when we have a party my teacher brings really gross snacks because most things that are in the stores I can't eat."

"Really gross? Sounds terrible." Lauren smiled as Jake continued to explain the extent of his disgust with his teacher's party fare.

Finally, she broke in, knowing she was being bamboozled into doing something she'd pretty much decided against—going over to Seth's house and cooking again. "Listen, Jake, I understand how you feel, but calling me without your father's permission is still wrong."

"I know, and I really am sorry, but the other kids all know we get gross treats because of me. Sometimes they say really mean things when the teacher can't hear. I thought maybe this time we could have normal snacks so the other kids won't be mad at me."

Yep. She'd been bamboozled. "Okay. I'll tell you what. I'll call your dad and see what he has to say. If he agrees, I'll come over."

"Thanks, Miss Lauren."

"Don't thank me until after I've called your dad."

"I think he'll say yes."

"Maybe. I'll let you know in a little bit."

She called Seth's cell phone and left a message on his machine, then pulled up a few menus that would work for Seth's class and for him. At least she thought they'd work. He'd had a reaction to something he'd eaten. Seth was so careful about his son's diet, it didn't seem possible that he would have allowed something into the house that triggered a reaction in Jake.

She'd have to ask. Sometimes new allergies could crop up as a person aged. Hopefully that wasn't the case with Jake. His diet was already limited enough. She'd choose her recipes based on the information she had. If that changed, she could easily make adjustments to the ingredients.

An hour later, her phone rang again.

Seth.

Her heart leaped, her pulse followed.

"Hello?"

"Lola? Seth. I got your message. I want to apologize for my son."

"There's no need. He already apologized."

"That doesn't excuse what he did."

"I know, but he's a sweet kid, and he didn't mean any harm. It didn't bother me."

"That's because you're a nice person, Lola."

Nice? That was a little too close to boring, predictable and dull. "Only sometimes."

He chuckled and she imagined his strawberry blond hair and easy smile, the way his eyes crinkled at the corners when he laughed. "Lola, you're nice all the time. That's why you've done way more for Jake than I paid for. I don't want you to spend any more of your vacation cooking for him."

"I'm a chef, Seth, cooking is what I love to do, especially when I'm cooking for someone who really appreciates it."

"Jake certainly does. For that matter, so do I."

"Then let me make him something to bring in Wednesday. It won't take much time, and Jake can work with me. That'll help him feel a little more in control of his diet and his life."

"Which can only be a good thing?"

"Of course. He's a lot like I used to be, Seth. A confidence boost will go a long way toward making him feel more sure of himself."

"All right. You win. When do you want to come?"

"The party is Wednesday. If we bake the stuff today, it'll keep until then. How about some time this afternoon?"

"I've got meetings until six."

Perfect. She could help Jake *and* avoid Seth. "I was thinking a little earlier would be better. Can you call the sitter and let her know I'll be over around four?"

"Sure. Reese will be there by then. She can help if you need it."

"Great."

"How's everything going over there?"

"Pretty good. Dee has been her normal organized self and already has people scheduled to come clean up the mess left last night."

"And you're in her place with the doors and windows locked?"

"Yes, Dad." She meant it as a joke, but Seth didn't laugh.

Instead his voice rumbled into her ear, warm and filled with promise. "There are a lot of things I'd like to be to you, Lola. Dad isn't one of them."

His words begged a response but Lauren wasn't in the mood to remind Seth of all the reasons why they couldn't be together. What would she say, after all? That he was interested in her now, but that eventually he'd realize she was just as dull as he'd thought her all those years ago.

She'd rather change the subject. "Did you talk to Ellen again today? Find out anything more about what she overheard?"

"Yes. She had nothing else to add, so I called Seth's pediatrician to check his blood type."

"And?"

"And it's AB negative."

"That's great news."

"I think it is. Red hair, green eyes, the same blood type. The evidence is compelling."

"But?"

"Nothing. I'm just going to have to take some more time to accept everything Ellen told me."

"I'm sorry all this happened. You've already been through a lot."

"Life has its share of trouble for everyone. Fortunately, God can help us get through it."

"True." She smiled, happy that Seth had accepted what she'd tried years ago to convince him of. Though he'd attended church when they were teens, he'd never been intent on living his life with purpose. It seemed that had changed in the time they'd been apart.

"There's something else that's true, Lola." His voice had

warmed again, the deep-South drawl melting her in a way no one else ever had.

"What's that?"

"No matter how much you avoid discussions about our relationship and no matter how much you deny that there's still something between us, you don't really believe it."

Okay. So he was right. She didn't believe it. She also didn't believe that "us" meant much more than a few shared meals, a kiss or two, promises that were bound to be broken. "I'm not denying that there's still chemistry between us. I just don't want to do anything about it."

"I think you do. I think you want exactly what I do—a second chance."

"You're wrong."

"Am I? I think you need to ask yourself that before you go back to Savannah and back to your life there. You need to decide if you're willing to take a chance on us again, or if you're going to turn your back on a good thing because you're afraid of being hurt again."

"And *I* think it would be better if we didn't have this discussion again."

"Then I won't mention it again. Until you're ready." The line went dead, and Lauren was left standing with the phone pressed to her ear, wondering what Seth would have said if she'd told him the truth—that she knew why he was attracted to her, and that it was all a lie. That her exciting life of travel and teaching was nothing more than a cover for the shy, timid woman that still lurked inside.

The boring woman. The one he'd turned his back on once. She didn't plan to give him a chance to do it again.

But maybe you should. Maybe this has been God's plan

*all along. Not to have you marry when you were young and
unsure, when every negative word that was said wounded
like a knife, but to give you time to grow and gain confidence.
Maybe the time wasn't right then. Maybe it is now. And
maybe denying that is denying God's desire for your life.*

The thoughts whispered through her mind, but she
forced them back. The last twenty-four hours had been difficult. She wasn't going to add soul-searching into the mix.
Whatever God wanted, she'd be open to it, but she'd decide
what that might be later.

She turned on the laptop, scanning her e-mail messages and the guest book entries that needed to be
accepted or denied. One caught and held her attention.
The sender anonymous.

"This can't be good." She muttered the words as she
read the input—

Magnolia College is a great school with great people,
but some of those people don't belong. Ask Cornell
Rutherford what he's been doing these past years. You
might be surprised at the answer.

Cornell Rutherford? She'd seen him at the Half Joe just
a few days ago. He'd been as staid and debonair as ever.
People respected him, maybe even liked him. What could
he possibly be doing that would cause someone to comment on it?

Lauren didn't know, but she had a feeling the police
would want to find out.

She dialed Detective Anderson's number, resigning
herself to another trip to the police station.

TWENTY-TWO

Lauren's meeting with Detective Anderson took longer than she'd thought it would, and she was running late, shoving a bite of an oversize taco into her mouth as she pulled into Seth's driveway. She swiped shredded cheese off her black T-shirt and grabbed a bag of ingredients from the backseat. She needed to move fast if she were going to get cookies and cupcakes done and be out of the house before Seth got home.

Jake raced outside as she stepped out of the car, his cheeks flushed and blotchy, his skin pale. "Hi, Miss Lauren! I was worried you were mad and weren't going to come."

"Why would I be mad?"

"Because I was rude to call and ask you to do something for free that you usually get paid for."

"I take it you spoke to your father." She handed Jake the bag of ingredients and finished the last bite of her taco. She wanted another. Maybe she'd have a cookie once they were done.

"He wasn't happy. I've lost my video game privileges for a week."

"That sounds like a reasonable punishment."

"I guess. It was that or call you and tell you not to come tonight. I picked losing the video games."

Lauren smiled and ruffled his hair. "I'm flattered."

"Yeah, well your cookies are the best I've ever had. I figured I'd rather have a couple of those than play the video game."

This time she laughed. Good to know her cooking was better than video games. "I don't know about my cookies being the best, but I do know that I'm with you on preferring them over video games. What do you say we get inside and get started? I brought enough ingredients to make two different kinds and some cupcakes."

"Really? My class is going to love them. Let's go," he grabbed her hand, and she allowed herself to be pulled toward the house. "Reese is already inside. She's got the bowls and stuff out."

"Perfect. Are you recovered from your allergic reaction?"

"Except for the blotchy skin." He blushed and the hives that covered his face and neck deepened in color.

"Did you guys ever figure out what caused it?"

"That's the other reason I lost my video game privileges." He sighed and shook his head, shaggy curls falling across his forehead.

If he were Lauren's son, she'd brush them away. Her heart ached with the thought, and with the knowledge that what she'd wanted so desperately to have with Seth, he'd decided he'd rather have with someone else.

"Did you eat something you weren't supposed to?"

"Someone brought a mix of candy to school. Everyone got to take some. I took some stuff I knew I could eat, but they were in the bag with other things. Chocolate and peanut butter candy and stuff."

"Oops."

"Yeah, Dad's told me not to do that before, so I'm on punishment. Reese, Miss Lauren is here." Jake called out as he stepped into the house, and Reese appeared, her blond hair silky smooth and sliding over her shoulders, her makeup flawless.

She met Lauren's eyes, something flashing in her gaze. Maybe she was uncomfortable having Lauren in the house while she was babysitting, or maybe she was worried about someone stepping in and filling her role. Whatever the case, Lauren wasn't about to back off and leave to make her happy. She'd told Jake she was going to make treats for the party Wednesday, and that's what she planned to do.

She pulled ingredients from the bag, setting them on the counter near a mixer. "Want to preheat the oven to 375, Jake?"

"Sure—"

"I'll do it. Seth really doesn't want Jake fooling with the oven."

"Turning it on isn't fooling with it, Reese. I'm sure Seth would agree."

"He's not here to ask, and I'm not willing to make that call. Jake isn't my child." *Or yours.*

She didn't finish the thought, but Lauren was sure it *was* what she was thinking. "True. I'll turn on the oven. Jake, can you put the beater on the mixer?"

"I'll handle that. Jake, go ahead and sit at the table so you're out of the way."

Was having Jake help worth fighting over?

Yeah. It was.

Lauren turned from the oven and faced Reese. "I agreed to make treats for Jake's class if he helped. When Seth and I spoke this morning, that was what was discussed."

"I see." Reese frowned. "I certainly don't mean to intrude on that. I'll just go in Seth's office and get some schoolwork done."

"You're welcome to stay and help if you want, Reese. The more the merrier."

"I thought it was Too many cooks spoil the soup." Reese smiled, the expression wan, her skin pale beneath her blush. Perfect makeup couldn't hide the circles under her eyes, and despite the young woman's obvious animosity, Lauren felt sorry for her.

"Good thing we aren't making soup." Lauren handed her a bar of baker's chocolate. "How about chopping this into chunks?"

She hesitated, then shook her head. "I really should get some work done."

She headed down the hall, and Lauren rubbed the tension in her neck. If the first five minutes of her visit were any indication, this was going to be a long hour or two.

She left at six-thirty, rushing out to her car, the scent of chocolate and vanilla clinging to her skin. Seth hadn't returned yet, and she didn't plan to run into him in the driveway. She needed more time to think about what he'd said, more time to decide what she wanted.

The sky was hazy with twilight, the evening air brisk with the first taste of fall. If she let herself, she could imagine sitting on the porch, a cup of coffee in her hand, waiting for Seth to come home. She could picture his deep, green eyes and the slight curve of his lips, the strong line of his jaw and the strength of his hands as they wrapped around her waist; the heat of his lips as they pressed against hers.

Whoa! Not a good thing to be imagining.

She pulled open the car door, dropped her laptop onto the backseat and started back toward Dee's house. She'd have to tell her sister about the e-mail she'd received today. Between the cleaners, the glass repairs, the visit to the police station and baking for Jake, Lauren had tried to contact her sister with little result. Obviously, Dee's day had been just as busy as hers.

Her head throbbed with tension as she headed back toward Dee's house. She was more tired and stressed now than she'd been in Savannah. Which just proved that vacations weren't all they were cracked up to be. Tonight she was going to do her best to put the troubles she'd run into behind her. First, a hot shower to wash away the scent of baking that clung to her. Then a good book and a bowl of hot, buttered popcorn.

By the time she pulled into Dee's empty driveway, Lauren was in a better mood. So things hadn't turned out quite the way she'd planned. This was still her vacation. No clients calling with emergencies that required six hours of cooking and two hours of cleanup. No one complaining that microwaving precooked chicken for twenty minutes had dried out the meal and made it inedible. She loved her job, but at the moment she didn't miss it. Maybe that was because she'd spent so much time cooking for Jake.

And Seth.

She headed for Dee's house, her laptop and purse in hand, visions of buttered popcorn and cold soda making her mouth water. Hopefully, her sister had remembered how much she loved popcorn and had it stocked in the kitchen. Otherwise, she'd have to go out to the carriage house to get the supply she'd brought with her.

The thought brought another. She'd planned to pack her suitcase and bring it to Dee's house. Lauren rounded the corner of the house and started across the yard. The cleaners had done a great job, and the door looked no different than it had before. Lauren still didn't want to touch it. Unfortunately, her clothes were on the other side.

She used the key, turned off the alarm and strode across the living room. The bedroom was just as she'd left it, her Bible on the nightstand, her makeup spread out on the dresser. It didn't take long to throw her clothes into the suitcase, toss her makeup into a bag and drag the whole lot back outside.

Maneuvering the suitcase across the yard with her laptop and purse in her hands was a little more time-consuming. The wheels of the suitcase caught on the stones and hunks of grass, the bumpy tug of it throwing her off balance as she walked. She yanked at the handle, pulling harder, trying to hurry.

A soft shuffle sounded from somewhere behind her. Shoes on grass, rustling as someone moved toward her.

Lauren turned, her heart slamming against her ribs, her pulse racing. Twilight hid little, the deep green of trees and branches, the lush thickness of the grass, the emptiness of the yard. There was nothing there. Not even a squirrel disturbed the manicured lawn and well-groomed garden. Her mind told her that, but her heart didn't believe it. The racing throb of her pulse echoed in her ears as she tugged at the suitcase again, her eyes scanning the yard for signs that someone was lurking just out of sight.

"Go home, Lauren. Before it's too late." The hissed whisper came from behind her, and Lauren whirled again, icy fear slushing through her veins.

No more phone calls. No more bricks with messages taped to them. This was the real thing. Terror in the flesh standing a few feet away. Black clothes. Black ski mask. Eyes glittering in the dim light. An arm's length away and standing between Lauren and the house.

"Who are you? What do you want?" Lauren took a step away, her heart thudding a sickening beat.

"I'm your last warning. Go home, Lauren. Before something terrible happens."

Male or female? Tall or short? Lauren couldn't tell. Twilight played tricks on the mind and the eyes, and she wasn't even sure that what she was seeing was real. "And if I do go home?"

Another step back.

And another.

This wasn't a benign visit. It wasn't a simple warning. Lauren knew it. She just needed a little more distance between them before she ran, a little more of a chance to make it to safety.

"There aren't any guarantees in life are there? But at least you won't have to worry about me."

"I don't understand why you're so determined to make me leave."

A third step. Now she was out of arm's reach. Far enough to turn her back and run.

If she dared.

"Because it's what I want. What I want, I get."

"Okay. I'll leave first thing in the morning." *Please let me live that long, Lord. I have so many things I still want to do. A whole life I still want to live.*

"No. You'll leave now." Before Lauren realized what was happening the figure lunged toward her, yanking at her purse and shoving hard, the force driving Lauren backward.

Don't lose your footing. Don't fall. If you do, you'll be like that poor woman under the sidewalk. Dead.

She managed to pivot, her ankle twisting as she shifted her weight and ran toward the trees and whatever safety they offered.

Faster. Run faster.

Branches snapped. Grass rustled. The sound of pursuit. Of danger. The hot breath of violence. Of hate.

Something slammed into her back, knocking her forward. Her head slammed against the trunk of a tree, stars dancing in front of her eyes as she jumped up again, ran again.

Pain. Sharp. Brutal. Cutting through her skull until it was all she knew. And then velvety darkness as she collapsed, the blackness welcoming her as she fell into oblivion.

TWENTY-THREE

Darkness.

Pain.

Nightmare.

Reality.

Lauren groaned, struggling to open her eyes and seeing nothing but blackness.

No, not blackness. Tiny stars sprinkled the night sky. The gibbous moon cast silvery light through the trees. Frogs croaked and called, their nightly serenade pounding into Lauren's head with the force of a sledgehammer. It hurt to move. It hurt to breathe.

But she was alive.

"Thank You, Lord." She moaned the prayer as she pushed up onto her knees, rocks and sticks gouging her hands, her head throbbing in time with her heartbeat.

She needed to get to her feet, get to the house, call for help, but her body was sluggish and unresponsive, and she stayed where she was. Not quite down. Not quite up.

"So get up, Lauren. You can't stay here all night." As pep talks went, hers was miserable, but Lauren pushed to her feet anyway.

Someone had attacked her. She wasn't going to lie out here waiting for him to come back.

And she wasn't going to let him get away with it.

She needed to call Detective Anderson.

She needed to get to the house.

She needed to *focus*.

One step at a time, back through the trees, back across the yard. Had an hour passed? Two? The lights in the house were off. Dee must still be at work.

Lauren's suitcase lay on the ground, unopened. Her purse and laptop…gone. Or maybe not. Maybe they were somewhere else, dropped in her mad dash to escape.

Somewhere in the distance a dog barked, sirens blared, and a motorcycle roared, but close to the house the world was silent, even the frogs quieting. A branch cracked and Lauren jumped, pain spearing through her skull until she wanted to vomit.

Was he still here? Had he been waiting all this time for her to wake?

She half jogged to the front of the house, her eyes tearing, her stomach clenching. This was pain. This was terror.

The door. Open the door. Where were the keys?

She checked her pockets, tried to remember what she'd done after she'd left the carriage house, but her mind was fuzzy, her thoughts muddled. The neighbor was close. Robertson. Robinson. Something like that. She just had to get to his house and she'd be safe.

She took a step away from the door, swayed, the world darkening as she grabbed the door handle and held on until the dizziness passed. Even then her legs were wobbly, her body weak.

Walking to the neighbor might not be an option, after all, but there was something else she could do.

She shuffled to the edge of the yard, picking up a large decorative rock. One, two…sorry, Dee…three. She slammed the rock against the window, breaking the glass. Slammed it again and again, tears streaming down her face, her head throbbing in agony, until the rock went through the window and the alarm shrieked its warning.

Done.

She collapsed onto the fragrant grass in front of the window, resting her head on her knees and praying the police would get there soon.

"Two kind of cookies *and* cupcakes?" Seth eyed the abundance of treats that lined the counter, and shot a look at his son. "Did you ask Lauren to make extra?"

"No, Dad. It was Miss Lauren's idea to make two kinds of cookies. Wasn't it, Reese?"

Reese grabbed her books from the kitchen table, and nodded. "It was, Seth. I told her you probably weren't going to approve, but she said you had an agreement."

"Actually, we did, so it's okay."

"Okay? She wanted Jake to turn on the stove. That's not okay in my book."

"He's ten, Reese. It's time for him to start learning some life skills."

"I know. She just…"

"What?"

"Seems determined to take things over." Her pale cheeks flushed, and she started toward the door. "Not that it's any of my business if you want her telling your son what to do."

"She doesn't really tell me what to do, Reese. She's just helping me learn to cook." Jake scowled, and Seth groaned inwardly.

This was not what he'd been hoping to come home to.

He'd been hoping to find Lauren in the kitchen, Jake at her side. Instead, he'd walked into jealousy and angst. "Jake, go pack your book bag for tomorrow."

"But—"

"Go. Now." Once his son ran up the stairs, Jake turned to Reese. "Sorry if Lauren stepped on your toes. It's got to be awkward having someone else working here while you're babysitting. I should have thought to ask her if she'd mind watching Jake until I got home. Then you could have had the evening off."

"That would have been unnecessary. You know how much I love being here with Jake."

"You do. And Jake loves spending time with you, but Lauren is able to offer him something that neither you nor I can—a chance to be accepted in school. You know how much he's struggled with that."

"Of course, I do." She smiled, the expression brittle. "And I didn't mean anything bad. Lauren is nice. I just wasn't sure how much mothering you wanted her to do when she's here."

"Since my son doesn't have memories of having a mother, whatever Lauren wants to give him is fine by me."

"But won't Jake be hurt when she goes back home?"

"Savannah isn't that far from here, Reese. I'm sure we'll be seeing more of Lauren after her vacation is over." He hoped they would anyway.

"You're right. I'm being silly. I just worry about Jake. He's so delicate."

"Not as delicate as he used to be." Seth walked to the door with her. "You still up for tomorrow? Or do you need some time off?"

"Of course I don't." She stepped outside. "This job is all that's standing between me and cafeteria food for dinner every night."

Seth laughed, waving as Reese got into her car.

There. That was settled. Now maybe he could relax. It had been a long day. Too long. He glanced at the clock. Eight-thirty. Still early, but it felt late. That's what he got for staying up until 2 a.m.

"Hey, Dad?" Jake called from the top of the stairs.

"Yes?"

"Why doesn't Reese like Miss Lauren?"

"Who says she doesn't?"

"No one, but she sure acts weird every time Miss Lauren comes over."

"It's just strange for her to have someone else telling you what to do. Did you guys have fun tonight?"

"We sure did. I learned how to zest a lemon."

"Did you?"

"Yep."

"And did you manage to get your homework done while all that fun was happening?"

Jake's pink cheeks revealed the truth before he even spoke.

"Go do it now before you run out of time."

"Okay." He started down the upstairs hall, but turned back to face Seth again. "Thanks for letting Lauren come today."

"No problem. Just make sure you don't ever call her again without permission."

"I won't. I promise."

He ran back toward his room, and Seth wandered back into the kitchen. The house felt empty tonight, the sweet scent of home-baked goods making Seth long for someone to share the evening with. Preferably someone with curly brown hair and vivid blue eyes.

His cell phone rang as he made himself a chicken sandwich, and he glanced at the number. Dee Owens.

"Hello?"

"Seth, it's Dee." The hoarse sound of her voice made his nerves go on high alert.

"What's wrong?"

"Lauren. Someone attacked her at the house. The police just called me. They're transporting her to the hospital."

Icy fear raced through his blood. "Is she okay?"

"I don't know. I'm trying to get to the hospital, but traffic is tight."

"Where are you?"

"Not close enough. I had a dinner meeting in Savannah tonight. I've called Kate, Cassie, Steff and Jennifer. They're on their way to meet the ambulance, but I think Lauren would want me to call you, too. If anything happens to her…"

"Nothing is going to happen to her. Lauren is tough. She'll be fine." And he was going to be at the hospital to make sure of it.

"I just wish I could be there faster."

"Go the speed limit. Getting into an accident and getting yourself killed isn't going to help Lauren. I'll see you in a while."

"Right."

Seth disconnected, dialed his neighbor and asked if she'd be willing to watch Jake, then called up the stairs.

"Jake, I've got to go out for a while. Mrs. Jefferson is coming. Go to bed on time and get that homework done."

"I will, Dad." Jake appeared at the top of the stairs again. "Is everything okay?"

"It will be. Come here." He wrapped his son in a bear hug, dropped a kiss on the top of his head. "Be good."

"I'm always good. Everyone says so."

"Then I guess I don't have to worry about it."

The doorbell rang, and Seth let Mrs. Jefferson in, everything inside of him screaming that he needed to leave *now.* "Thanks for coming on such short notice."

"I've got sixteen busy grandkids, Seth. Watching your lone son is never a problem. You just take your time and make sure your friend is okay. I'll look after Jake."

Seth nodded, unable to speak past his anger and fear. Lauren. He had to get to her.

He managed to find a parking spot at the hospital, and he sprinted to the emergency room entrance. Dee wasn't there yet, but Cassie, Steff and Jennifer were.

When they saw him, they moved as a group, their shocked expressions mirroring Seth's feelings.

"Is she okay?"

"We don't know. They're checking her out now. The receptionist said it was a head injury, though." Steff rubbed her neck, her expression grim.

"That doesn't sound good."

"No, it doesn't." Cassie's normal perkiness was gone, her skin leached of color, her face stark against the background of bright red hair.

"I'm going to see what I can find out." Seth walked to the receptionist.

"Can I help you?"

"I'm trying to find out information on Lauren Owens."

She glanced at a computer screen, nodded. "They just brought her in. I don't know much more than that."

"Can I see her?"

"Are you family?"

"A close friend." Sort of. "Her sister is on the way, but asked me to come. She didn't want Lauren to be alone."

"Usually we don't let anyone but family back in the treatment area."

But she was waffling, Seth could tell. "I understand, but Lauren might feel better if someone she knows is with her."

"All right. She's in triage room five. Go on back."

"Thanks." He sent a quick wave in Jennifer, Steff and Cassie's direction and hurried down the corridor. The fact that the receptionist let him go had to mean Lauren was okay. At least he hoped that's what it meant. Losing her now, when he was just getting to know her again, was something he didn't even want to contemplate.

The door to triage five was open, and Seth walked in, his gaze riveted on the gurney in the center of the room. Lauren lay there, her eyes closed, her forehead bloody.

"Lola?"

Her eyes opened slowly, as if she were in a dream and not quite able to wake. "Seth. What are you doing here? Where's Jake?"

"I'm here because I was worried. Jake is home with a sitter."

"You didn't need to worry. I'm okay."

"You don't look okay." He stepped close, his stomach clenching with fury as he took in her scratched face, her tangled hair. He tamped it down, reaching for her hand, running his thumb over her knuckles. "Who did this to you, babe?"

"Someone who knew me. Knew my name. And wants me to go home."

"He beat you up?" Or had something worse happened? Something Seth didn't even want to think about.

"Threatened me. Then knocked me out."

"If I find out who it is—"

"You'll tell the police and let them deal with it." She smiled, winced and closed her eyes. "I've got the dickens of a headache, Seth. Do you think you can get me some Tylenol?"

"I'd get you the moon if you asked." He stroked her hair, letting his fingers tangle in the mass of curls spread out on the white gurney cover.

She smiled, opening her eyes again, staring into his. "The moon? That's quite a line, Seth."

"It did its job."

"Which was?"

"To make you smile."

"You could always do that. Remember all those times in high school when I was scared of doing an oral report, or nervous about starting a new class. You always found a way to make me feel better."

He had. Until he'd decided she wasn't the kind of woman he wanted. Then he'd turned his back on five years of shared dreams and late-night conversations.

What had he been thinking?

He hadn't.

But he was now, and he knew Lauren was his perfect

match, exactly the kind of woman he needed in his life. "It's what you deserved. You were the best part of my teenage years, Lola. The best part of college." He lifted her hand, kissed the soft skin of her palm. "I'm going to find a nurse and see if you can have something for the pain."

"She'll be back in a minute. I guess I can wait if that means you stay here with me." Her hand wrapped around his, holding him in place, her eyes so bright, so clear, Seth thought he could see to her very soul.

"I'll stay as long as you need me."

She smiled, her pallid cheeks regaining some of their color, and Seth knew he'd be happy to stay with her forever if she let him.

TWENTY-FOUR

Lauren still had a headache the following morning. A mild concussion was the doctor's assessment. Dee and Seth had both wanted her to stay at the hospital overnight, but Lauren couldn't stomach the thought of being alone. Anyone could have wandered into her hospital room.

She shuddered, easing up in her bed and trying to decide if she had the energy to get up.

"How are you doing?" Dee peered into the room, her hair tousled, her eyes dark with fatigue. Apparently, she didn't have much energy, either.

"Better."

"Good. I'm going to drive you back to Savannah this afternoon."

"You're kidding, right?"

"Wrong. Someone around here wants you to leave badly enough to attack you. You're going."

"I was going back Friday anyway. A couple of days more isn't going to hurt."

"A couple days more could be the difference between life and death."

"I think that's a little dramatic, Dee."

"I can't believe you're saying that after what happened last night."

"Yeah? Well at least if I stay here, I'll be with you. Once I get to Savannah, I'll be alone. Just because I was told I'd be safe if I left, doesn't mean I will be."

Dee hurried across the room and put her arm around Lauren's shoulder. "You're right, Lauren. I'm just panicking. You can stay with me as long as you want."

"Just until I can drive myself home. The doctor said Friday, right?" She was still a little fuzzy about the previous night's events. The only vivid memory she had was of Seth, lifting her hand, kissing her palm, his eyes ocean-green and worth drowning in.

She'd wanted him to stay. She wished he were here.

"I'm going to take the rest of the week off. We can hang out together while you recover and the police work on finding the guy who did this."

"You don't have to do that, Dee."

"Of course I do. You're my baby sister."

"Baby sister? There's barely a year between us." They'd been having this conversation since they were kids, and the familiarity of it was comforting. She'd been attacked and threatened, but she was okay. In time, her terror would fade and she'd go on with her life. For now, she'd accept Dee's help and be happy for it.

"Yes. Baby sister. The best one I've got."

"The only one you've got."

"That's why I'm taking the rest of the week off. Any work that needs doing can be done at home. So, how about some breakfast?"

"My head is pounding too badly to eat."

Concern etched thin lines in Dee's forehead. "I don't think I've ever known you to turn down a meal. I'm going to call the doctor and make sure this is normal."

"It's normal and I'm fine. I'll just rest for a while. Then I'll have something to eat." Lauren's strained smile must have been convincing.

Dee nodded, pulled heavy curtains over the window. "If you need something, just shout."

The door closed, the room falling into darkness. Every corner came alive, every shadow took on shape and substance. She closed her eyes, saw him again. The shadowman. His hard, glittering gaze. His stiff carriage.

Did she know him?

Detective Anderson had asked her that over and over again. Lauren had been asking herself the same thing. Whoever it was had said her name, but did that mean she knew him? His voice had been like a serpent's hiss, and when she closed her eyes she could hear it again, but it wasn't a voice she'd ever heard before.

She sighed, reaching for the bottle of Tylenol Dee had left on the bedside table the previous night and swallowing three with water. The house had fallen silent, Dee so quiet, Lauren thought about calling for her just to make sure she was still in the house.

That was silly.

Of course she was still in the house.

Lauren knew that, but knowing it didn't keep the fear from stealing up inside her and lodging beneath her sternum so that she could barely breathe.

"Laur?" Dee opened the door, temporarily freeing

her from the terror. "I've got something for you." She moved into the room, a large vase of pink and white roses in her hands.

"You bought me flowers?" Lauren sat up, wincing a little as Dee set the vase on the nightstand.

"Do you think they'd be roses if I had? Read the card."

Lauren lifted it, forcing her eyes to focus on the letters. "'You didn't ask for the moon, so I got you these instead. Always, Seth.'"

"Now that's a romantic guy. I think you should keep him."

Dee stepped out of the room again, and Lauren turned on her side, staring at the bright array.

Keep Seth? She didn't have him. She'd never had him. At least not as much as he'd had her. Her heart, her dreams, everything she'd wanted when she'd been young seemed to have been wrapped up in him. She wasn't sure she wanted to do that again.

She wasn't sure she *didn't* want to do it again.

Dee was right. The flowers were beautiful, the card was romantic. After eleven years apart, Seth still had the ability to move her, to touch that spot deep inside that no one else had ever gotten close to. For now, that was enough.

Lauren smiled, letting her head sink into the pillow and staring at the roses until sleep claimed her again.

By Wednesday afternoon, she was feeling more herself and was ready to be out of the house. Unfortunately, Dee had other ideas. Instead of sitting down to a thick hamburger or a slice of pizza, Lauren was ensconced on Dee's couch, a blanket over her knees and a bowl of oatmeal on a tray in front of her.

"You made this oatmeal yourself?" Lauren jabbed at the chunky goo.

"Yes. And it's good, so stop making faces at it."

"I'm not making faces, I'm contemplating."

"What?"

"My fate if I eat it."

"Brat." Dee tossed a pillow at Lauren. "Here I slaved over the stove for you, and you act like I'm serving you poison."

"No, I'm just remembering that time in ninth grade when you decided you were going to show me up by making Mom and Dad a gourmet dinner. The Chicken Cordon Bleu was hard enough to crack teeth."

"I overcooked it a little. And I wasn't trying to show you up."

"Sure you were. Just like I was trying to show you up when I tried out for cheerleading." A disaster that had caused her no end of mortification.

"I always wondered about that."

The phone rang and Dee grabbed it, the amusement in her eyes fading as she listened to the speaker. "Okay. I'll tell her. Thanks."

"Tell me what?"

"A couple of kids found your purse on the side of the road and turned it in. Detective Anderson said your cell phone, keys and wallet were still in it."

"Has my laptop shown up?"

"No, but he's hopeful that'll be found, too. He's also hoping to get some forensic evidence from your purse."

"I'm not going to hold my breath."

"Me, neither." The phone rang again, and Dee grabbed

it. "Hello? Hi." Her gaze flew to Lauren. "Hold on. She's right here."

She handed the phone to Lauren, her eyes wide and filled with worry. "It's Seth. Something happened to Jake. Something to do with cookies."

"Seth? What's going on?"

"I'm at the hospital. Jake went into anaphylactic shock at school. They gave him two shots of epinephrine, and he's stabilized, but things were touch and go for a few minutes."

"Thank the Lord he's okay. Do you know what he ate?"

"His teacher said it happened right after he ate one of the cookies you made."

Lauren went cold at his words. "No way. There was nothing in them that he was allergic to."

"Could they have come in contact with something? Maybe you were carrying walnuts in the same bag as the chocolate?"

"You know better than that, Seth." She pushed the blanket off her legs and stood, her head starting renewed throbbing.

"You're right. I do. I just can't understand it, Lola. One minute he was fine. The next he was gasping for breath."

"Do you have any of the cookies with you?"

"The teacher sent some with the ambulance driver."

"Keep them. I'll be there in about twenty minutes." She hung up. Not giving him a chance to argue. She was going. No matter what he said.

"What's going on? Where are you planning to go?"

"The hospital. Jake had a severe allergic reaction to the cookies he brought to school."

"That's terrible."

"It's worse than you think. I made the cookies."

"No way, Lauren. I know you. You'd never make a mistake like that."

"We'll see when I get to the hospital." She grabbed her jacket, remembered that she didn't have keys or a license. "I'm going to have to take your car."

"You're going to have to ride in it. There's no way I'm letting you drive."

That was fine by Lauren. She didn't care how she got to the hospital as long as she got there.

It took less than twenty minutes to get to the hospital, but it seemed longer to Lauren, every mile, every minute double what it should have been.

Dee pulled up in front of the emergency room entrance, and Lauren barely waited for the car to stop before she jumped out. The thought of Jake eating something she'd made, trusting completely in her and then becoming so desperately ill made her sick, her pounding head and churning stomach a terrible echo of the fear that was in her heart.

He could have died.

If he had, would it have been her fault, some error that she'd made that had caused it? She needed to see the cookies, taste them, find out if something was in them that shouldn't be.

By the time she stepped into the emergency room, Jake had been admitted, and a nurse directed Lauren to a small room on the pediatric floor. She knocked once, then pushed the door open.

Seth was there, standing over the hospital bed, his brow furrowed. He looked up as she walked in, his eyes speaking words he didn't say—welcome home.

"How is he?" She whispered the words, not wanting to wake Jake if he'd fallen asleep.

"Better." Seth gestured her over, wrapping his arms around her waist and pulling her close. His heart beat beneath her ear, hard and frantic, as if he'd run a race and had yet to recover.

Lauren burrowed closer, her gaze on the bed and the young boy who lay there. Pale. Wan. Eyes closed. An oxygen mask over his face. Jake looked frail and ill, and Lauren nearly choked with the sorrow of it.

"Hey, it's okay." Seth wiped a tear from her cheek, his fingers lingering on her flesh, the contact shivering through her.

"No, it's not. Look at him. He's completely helpless."

"Not completely. He's got us here to look after him."

Us. A team working together to make sure Jake was taken care of. The thought warmed her and she nodded, the throbbing pain in her head making her sway forward.

Back into Seth's arms.

Where she belonged.

For once, she didn't push aside the thought, didn't try to deny the feeling.

"You're pale." He cupped her jaw, his thumb caressing her cheek. "Sit down. Let me get you some water."

"You've got enough to worry about without adding me to the list."

"Add? You were already on it." He smiled, weaving his fingers through her hair and leaning close. "How's the bump?"

"Big as a goose egg."

"And the headache?"

"The same."

He frowned, backing her toward the window and the chair beneath it. "You should be in bed."

"I needed to be here." With Jake. With you. "Do you have the cookies?"

"Yes, and I'll give them to you as soon as you take a seat."

"Bribery?"

"Whatever works." He leaned down, pressed a kiss to her lips, the contact gentle as spring rain.

"What was that for?"

"You. Me." He shrugged. "Us."

There was that word again.

The more she heard it, the more it seemed to fit.

She sat in the chair, taking the container of cookies Seth offered.

They weren't hers. She knew it immediately. She'd used chunks of baker's chocolate. Not chocolate chips. "I didn't make these."

"They were on the counter this morning. I handed them to Jake as he walked out the door."

"They might have been on your counter, but I didn't make them." She lifted one, bit into it. "I think there are walnuts in them."

Jake pulled one out of the container and broke it apart over a napkin. "You're right. I can see some. They're small but there."

"Someone brought them into your house, Seth. I never would have done such a thing."

"You don't have to tell me that. I already know it." He pulled her to her feet, wrapped her in his arms. "You're the best person I know, Lola. I can't believe I ever pushed you out of my life."

She snuggled close for a moment, enjoying his warmth, his strength. "I can't believe I ever let you. Now, let me go and call the police. I think they need to know about this."

"I think you're right." As he spoke, the door flew open and Reese raced in, her eyes wild, her hair flying around her face.

"Is he okay? Tell me he's going to be okay."

"He's going to be fine. The doctors are just keeping him overnight for observation."

"When I got your message I was sick about it. This is all my fault. I'm such an idiot." She was sobbing uncontrollably, and Seth sent a confused glance in Lauren's direction.

Lauren patted the younger woman's shoulder, handed her a tissue. "It's not your fault, and you're not an idiot. Someone switched the cookies I made."

She shrugged away from Lauren's hand, her eyes blazing with fury. "Don't you get it? *I* switched the cookies before I left last night."

"What?!" Seth's hands fisted, his eyes shimmering green fire.

"Jake was in bed. He wasn't going to eat any, so I thought it would be fine. He'd asked me to bring them up to the school at the end of the day so they'd be a last-minute surprise for his class. I planned to notice the nuts in them before I handed them out. Then make sure Jake didn't eat any."

"Why?" Seth's fury seeped into the word, harsh, violent, and Lauren put a hand on his arm.

"Why do you think? I was tired of Lauren getting between us. I thought Jake's teacher would tell you what had almost happened, and you'd be upset with her, send her packing and out of your life. I never meant for Jake to eat the cookies. How was I supposed to know you'd tell him to bring them to school himself?" She was sobbing so loudly, Lauren thought she might wake Jake.

"You need to calm down, Reese. If Jake wakes up he'll be terrified."

"You need to shut up and stay out of this. Everything that happened is your fault. You shouldn't stick your nose into other people's lives."

The words were so familiar a chill raced up Lauren's spine. "You're the one who's been threatening me."

"I wouldn't have had to if you'd just gone home and left us all alone."

Seth's muscles tensed, his glower causing Reese to sink down into the chair. "Lauren, call the police."

"The police?" Reese's sobs rose to hysterics. "I told you I didn't mean to hurt Jake. It was an accident."

"You can explain it to the police when they get here." Seth sounded weary, and Lauren wrapped her arm around his waist, offering him support.

"But you don't understand, Seth. I've spent two and a half years taking care of you and Jake. Then she came into the picture and everything changed."

"Nothing changed, Reese. You were still Jake's baby-sitter. You were still part of our lives."

"But I wanted more. I thought you wanted more."

Seth shook his head, backing away from the young woman. "Then you had the wrong idea."

"I'm so, so sorry."

She continued to cry until Detective Anderson strode into the room and escorted her away.

TWENTY-FIVE

Jealousy was a powerful motivator. Lauren had always known it, but witnessing what it had done to Reese only reinforced the knowledge. Once a college student, now a criminal. It hadn't taken her long to admit it. Half an hour after Detective Anderson had brought her in for questioning, she'd admitted to trashing the guesthouse, making threats over the phone and throwing a brick through the guesthouse window. She also admitted to switching the cookies in the hopes of ruining Lauren's reputation. Unfortunately, she'd almost killed Jake in the process.

"You're deep in thought. Want to share?" Seth's lips brushed the tender flesh behind her ear, his hand squeezing hers beneath the table he'd reserved at Terra Cottage. A posh Italian restaurant, it had a romantic ambience, the intimate tables making it easy to feel as if they were alone on their first official date since their official breakup.

A date.

The thought made Lauren smile. "I was thinking about Reese and the mess she made for herself."

"And I've been thinking about you." His lips trailed from her ear to her jaw, sending shivers of longing through her.

"Seriously."

"I'm very serious."

"So am I."

He backed away, looking into her eyes, making her want to forget about Reese and everyone else for that matter. "What's got you worried, Lola?"

"It just seems strange that a woman like Reese would be so crazy with jealousy."

"A woman like Reese? I suppose you mean something by that."

"Just that she seemed so together, so confident. Not the kind of person who'd put all her hopes into a man and then go crazy when things didn't work out."

"I see your point. I never would have suspected Reese of something like this, either, but she's admitted to everything."

"Not everything. She didn't admit to attacking me. She didn't admit to the blood on the door. What if it wasn't her?"

"Who else would it be?"

"I don't know. I just keep thinking that some of what's happened lately has to do with my work on the Web site."

"If there's a connection Detective Anderson will find it. Right now, he's pretty certain that Reese hired someone to attack you. She had an alibi, but that doesn't mean she wasn't involved. The lie detector test she took proved that she wasn't telling the truth when she said she knew nothing about it." He traced the curve of her arm, laced his fingers through hers.

"I know. I just feel like this isn't over."

"It isn't. Not until the police find the person who hurt you, but I do think you're safe again."

"You're right. I know you are, I'm just…"

"A worrier, but you don't have to worry anymore. Reese was the driving force behind everything. With her behind bars, there's no reason for her accomplice to continue what she started."

"It's all so sad and dark. The obsession with you and Jake. The jealousy. I'd almost feel sorry for Reese if she hadn't nearly killed Jake."

"That's exactly why I don't want to waste any more time talking about her, so let's talk about something else." He skimmed a finger over her lips, his gaze so intense, she blushed.

"Like?" Her heart slowed, her blood seeming to thicken in her veins.

"Those e-mails you were getting."

She smiled and shook her head. "And here I thought you wanted to talk about us."

"That, too, but the e-mails first. When Reese took the lie detector test she told the truth about not sending them, but lied when she said she knew nothing about the matter."

"You think she knows about something that's going on at the college? That maybe one of her friends is involved in this?"

"I don't think anything. Detective Anderson does. He's doing all he can to get a name from Reese, but she's not talking. She's probably protecting the person."

"Or worried that if she talks the person she hired will come after her." A picture of the shadowy figure popped into Lauren's head and she shivered.

"Cold?"

"Just wishing none of this had happened."

"None of it?" He traced circles on the inner curve of her

elbow, leaning close enough for her to see the specks of gold and blue in his eyes, close enough for her to feel the warmth of his body and the strength of his arm. She felt breathless with it. With him.

"I haven't decided yet."

"No? Is there anything I can do to convince you?"

"Probably not."

"What are you afraid of, Lola? Besides being hurt again."

"That you think I'm something I'm not. That you look at me and see an exciting woman who's traveled the world. A woman who is what you were looking for when you walked away from me eleven years ago."

"Would that be so wrong?" He smoothed her hair, his fingers playing with a curl that lay on her shoulder, the gentle caress speeding her pulse.

"No, but it's not who I am. If you think it is, you're only going to be disappointed." Again. She didn't say the word, but it was there.

"Then let me tell you who I think you are. You're a woman who can make my heart melt with a glance, a woman whose faith inspires me and whose compassion makes me look at the world in a different way. A woman who makes decisions with her heart *and* her head. A woman I want in my life."

"You're full of sweet words, Seth, but I've heard them before. We planned a whole life together, but in the end I wasn't what you wanted."

"I was too young to know what I wanted, Lola. So were you. If we'd married a decade ago, would we still be together now? I wonder."

"I've wondered the same thing. Maybe the timing

wasn't right when we were younger. Maybe staying together wasn't part of God's plan for either of our lives. Maybe a million things, but how can I know?"

"You don't have to know. You just have to have faith. In God. In yourself. In me. Can you do that? If you can, the rest will be easy."

Faith. Walking forward into the unknown with confidence that God would make everything work out in His perfect way and perfect time. Could she do it? Did she want to?

She stared into Seth's eyes, searching for answers and finding them in the quiet patience of his gaze. There was no rush, no hurry, just the simple desire to be with her. She smiled, pulled his head toward hers. "I think I can give it a try."

Their lips met, their dreams uniting once again. White picket fences. Cookies in the oven. Love. Lauren couldn't be sure of what the next weeks, months and years would hold, but she trusted that God was in control of them and that no matter what happened, Seth would be there. Friend. Companion. Love of her life. All she'd ever hoped for, all she'd ever dreamed of.

She smiled as he took her hand and pulled her to her feet.

"Let's get out of here."

"And go where?"

"Does it matter as long as we're together?"

Lauren laughed, walking out of Terra Cottage, Seth's hand wrapped around hers as they stepped into the future together.

EPILOGUE

They walked out of the restaurant hand in hand. Lauren and Seth Chartrand, staring into each other's eyes, so besotted with each other they didn't notice the shadow cast on the sidewalk near Seth's car. Even if they had, they wouldn't have known its significance or noticed that someone was standing near the streetlight.

Watching.

Waiting.

Things should have been over a week ago. Lauren should have gone back to her life and stopped digging into the past. Maybe now she would. Love could be a powerful distraction.

Only time would tell.

For now there was nothing to do but wait and watch.

Action was preferable, but action couldn't be taken without consequences. One person knocked on the head and the entire police force was combing the streets asking questions. Fortunately the girl had been the perfect scapegoat.

Everything would be fine as long as she didn't talk. One hint that she was going to, one whisper or rumor, and things would change.

There were other construction sites. Other dark nights. Other places where bodies could be hidden and not be found for a decade.

Patience. That's what the situation called for.

Action would come later.

* * * * *

Don't miss the next thrilling installment in the
REUNION REVELATIONS *series,*
DON'T LOOK BACK by Margaret Daley.
Available March 2008.

Dear Reader,

My college days were filled with friends with whom I've since lost touch. There is one friend, though, who has remained in my life. Darlene is like a fourth sister. When I was asked to write the second book in the Magnolia Falls continuity, I immediately thought about my relationship with her. I also began to wonder about people I hadn't heard from in years, women and men with whom I had become quite close during college, but had lost touch with after graduation. Because of that, it was easy for me to step into Lauren's shoes, to imagine what she was thinking and feeling as she reconnected with a man she'd once loved and searched for friends she'd once cared deeply about.

MISSING PERSONS is a story about those things and more. It is a story about betrayal, forgiveness, love. Most of all, it is a story of faith—renewed, reinvigorated, refreshed. And that, I think, is something we all need.

Enjoy!

Blessings,

Shirlee McCoy

QUESTIONS FOR DISCUSSION

1. Lauren is worried about seeing Seth again. Though she'd like to believe she's over him, she's not quite sure it's true. How has their past relationship influenced her life and the decisions she's made?

2. What is it that Seth is reminded of when he sees Lauren again? How do the memories of who she was mesh with the reality of who she has become?

3. Seth's son, Jake, has severe food allergies. His awkward shyness reminds Lauren of herself when she was a child. Because of that, she wants to help him despite her desire to keep her distance from Seth. Based on her personality, does her decision seem reasonable? Why or why not?

4. Someone's body was found buried on the Magnolia College campus. Lauren is worried about who it might be. Seth is terrified the remains might be those of his sister. Their shared concern draws them together, but more than that holds them there. What is it that draws them toward each other even as they both try to find reasons to stay apart?

5. Forgiveness isn't always easy. Though we want to follow Christ's example and His command, we often find it hard to rid ourselves of hard feelings. Is Lauren able to forgive Seth? Describe an instance when you had a hard time forgiving someone.

6. Forgiveness doesn't always mean reconciliation. Sometimes it only means letting go of anger and resentment. Sometimes, though, God asks us for more. In Lauren's case, what does she feel God telling her? Is she happy about it? What is her initial response? How do her feelings change as the story progresses?

7. Seth's feelings and opinions about Lauren change during the course of the story. What is it about her that intrigues him most? How does he feel about the part he's played in the woman she's become?

8. In life, we don't always get second chances. Seth and Lauren are blessed that they do. Is there a relationship in your life that is broken? Is there a path that might lead to a second chance and reconciliation?

9. God is not the author of confusion, but sometimes our emotions get in the way of knowing the truth of what He desires. In your relationships, are there issues you're praying about, paths you're considering but that you can find no peace about? What are God's promises to us regarding faith, love and mercy? How can these things guide you as you continue to seek His will? How did they guide Lauren as she struggled with her feelings for Seth?

10. Lauren worked hard to overcome shyness so that she could be successful in her business. Despite her success and her hard-won self-confidence, she still must force herself to be part of social events. Is Lauren's experi-

ence indicative of most people's? Is it possible to truly leave the past behind, or will what we were always influence who we are and what we've become?

INTRODUCING

Love Inspired

HISTORICAL

A NEW TWO-BOOK SERIES.

Every month, acclaimed
inspirational authors
will bring you engaging stories
rich with romance, adventure
and faith set in a variety
of vivid historical times.

History begins on **February 12**
wherever you buy books.

Steeple
Hill®

www.SteepleHill.com

REQUEST YOUR FREE BOOKS!
2 FREE RIVETING INSPIRATIONAL NOVELS PLUS 2 FREE MYSTERY GIFTS

Love Inspired®
SUSPENSE

YES! Please send me 2 FREE Love Inspired® Suspense novels and my 2 FREE mystery gifts. After receiving them, if I don't wish to receive any more books, I can return the shipping statement marked "cancel." If I don't cancel, I will receive 4 brand-new novels every month and be billed just $3.99 per book in the U.S. or $4.74 per book in Canada, plus 25¢ shipping and handling per book and applicable taxes, if any*. That's a savings of 20% off the cover price! I understand that accepting the 2 free books and gifts places me under no obligation to buy anything. I can always return a shipment and cancel at any time. Even if I never buy another book from Steeple Hill, the two free books and gifts are mine to keep forever.

123 IDN EL5H 323 IDN ELQH

Name	(PLEASE PRINT)	
Address		Apt. #
City	State/Prov.	Zip/Postal Code

Signature (if under 18, a parent or guardian must sign)

Order online at www.LoveInspiredSuspense.com

Or mail to Steeple Hill Reader Service™:

IN U.S.A.: P.O. Box 1867, Buffalo, NY 14240-1867
IN CANADA: P.O. Box 609, Fort Erie, Ontario L2A 5X3

Not valid to current Love Inspired Suspense subscribers.

Want to try two free books from another series?
Call 1-800-873-8635 or visit www.morefreebooks.com

* Terms and prices subject to change without notice. NY residents add applicable sales tax. Canadian residents will be charged applicable provincial taxes and GST. This offer is limited to one order per household. All orders subject to approval. Credit or debit balances in a customer's account(s) may be offset by any other outstanding balance owed by or to the customer. Please allow 4 to 6 weeks for delivery.

Your Privacy: Steeple Hill is committed to protecting your privacy. Our Privacy Policy is available online at www.eHarlequin.com or upon request from the Reader Service. From time to time we make our lists of customers available to reputable firms who may have a product or service of interest to you. If you would prefer we not share your name and address, please check here. ☐

Love Inspired® SUSPENSE

TITLES AVAILABLE NEXT MONTH

Don't miss these four stories in March

WILDFIRE by Roxanne Rustand
Snow Canyon Ranch

Years ago, Josh Bryant broke Tessa McAllister's heart. When he showed up again in *her* town, Tessa counted the days until he'd leave. She had enough to handle with drought, wildfire and underhanded rivals—she couldn't bear to risk her heart again.

DON'T LOOK BACK by Margaret Daley
Reunion Revelations

Cassie Winters was overjoyed when her brother got a job as a journalist...until his latest story resulted in a fatal end. Determined to find the truth, Cassie sought help from her former professor—and not-so-former crush—Jameson King.

BROKEN LULLABY by Pamela Tracy

Growing up in the Mob had left Mary Graham with emotional scars. Still, after years in hiding, Mary had nowhere to go but home. Home offered little safety, though, and fear soon drove Mary to turn to the last man *anyone* in her family could trust—policeman Mitch Williams.

MIA: MISSING IN ATLANTA by Debby Giusti

Finally home, returning war hero Jude Walker was ready to reunite with the woman he'd met on his last leave. Her last known address, though, was a homeless shelter. Shelter director Sarah Montgomery wanted to help, but she feared it would all end in heartache...for *both* of them.

LISCNM0208